"Just stay calm," Margaret said. "People don't get killed for their apartments." The light was about to change, and as Margaret took Thelma's arm to cross the street, a last car sped up to make the crossing. Thelma stepped out into the street at the same moment that Margaret screamed. . . .

A thin silver object skimmed by with incredible speed only a foot away. It hit ten yards up the block and kept bouncing and rolling until it crashed into a trash can, knocking it over. A young woman who was also waiting to cross came over to help.

"Hubcap," she said shaking her head. "Those things can be lethal. Car must have hit a bump."

Thelma took a deep breath, watching the car speed downtown. "Yes," she said. "Must have been a freak accident." But she looked at the smooth roadway and frowned at Margaret. Together they crossed the street, and when they were on the other side, Margaret whispered, "I'll speak to Lieutenant Morley tomorrow."

Thelma stared at her friend. "You don't think. . . ?"

Margaret nodded. "I saw him throw it!"

THE
CONDO
KILL

A Margaret Binton Mystery

Richard Barth

FAWCETT CREST • NEW YORK

For Katherine Sara

A Fawcett Crest Book
Published by Ballantine Books
Copyright © 1985 by Richard Barth

All rights reserved under International and Pan-American Copyright Conventions. Published in the United States by Ballantine Books, a division of Random House, Inc., New York, and simultaneously in Canada by Random House of Canada Limited, Toronto. Originally published by Charles Scribner's Sons in 1985.

Library of Congress Catalog Card Number: 85-14567

ISBN 0-449-21812-0

Manufactured in the United States of America

First Ballantine Books Edition: April 1991

One

"BINGO!" THE MAN AT THE NEXT TABLE said.

"Damn." Margaret Binton looked up and her flowery little hat quivered with her exasperation. She almost had it, everything but the bottom right corner of the X. While she had waited, seven numbers had been called. Lord, why do I ever do this? she asked herself and watched the man bring his card to the rostrum to be checked. I go through a pack of cigarettes a night, and the only thing I ever get is palpitations. Upending her card and sliding the markers into the little cup, she turned to look at the big clock on the side wall. Still, it was better than a night alone with the television set or with another detective novel, much as she enjoyed them. It was 9:15 which meant one last game—the full card and the worst of all. It took forever and always sent her home empty-handed and in a sweat. Rubbing the two cards together, she then set them back out on the table in front of her. She spit lightly on her thumb for luck and looked around the church basement while she waited for the first numbers to be called. Her eyes came to rest on the woman next to her.

"Thelma, switch seats," she whispered. Thelma lifted her head slowly and raised an eyebrow. Whatever wrinkles that action created were lost in the others already on her face. Her deeply dyed red hair looked as if it had been spun on top of her head like cotton candy while Margaret's gray hair

1

was drawn back in a neat little bun. She looked back at Margaret, but her attention seemed to be somewhere else.

"Switch seats," Margaret repeated. "Neither of us has won anything all night. Maybe it will change our luck."

Thelma shrugged, and got up silently, slid her one card along the table, and sat back down. By the time Margaret was repositioned with cards, chips, cigarettes, matches, ashtray, and pocketbook in front of her, the first numbered ball had fallen into the chute.

"O-73."

Margaret smiled and placed a marker on the top row of her right card. "I told you," she said and glanced at her friend's card. "You have it, too." Thelma nodded absently and placed a marker over the O-73. "That's a good omen," Margaret said. "One of us is going to win. I can feel it."

They weren't playing genteel bingo. The church's influence stopped short of the basement, and the cut-throat pace slackened only when the first player to yell "bingo" won the pot. It didn't matter if you were a split second late with a correctly filled card. On the other hand, if you were overzealous and yelled prematurely, you were out of the game. It made for a lot of excitement.

Twenty-five minutes later Margaret had gone through four cigarettes and a half-dozen Kleenex tissues. The area under her eyes was damp with perspiration, and her back ached from bending over her cards.

"G-54."

"Damn," she muttered and held her breath for three seconds. Her sigh mingled with those of the seventy-five other players.

"N—"

A lifetime went by in silence. The caller stopped impishly for a drink of water. The hairs on the back of Margaret's neck stood up, and she closed her eyes. N-34, she pleaded silently—her last number to win.

"—33."

Margaret gritted her teeth. Three seconds passed, then

four, then five. She lit another cigarette and leaned over toward Thelma.

"It's amazing that more people don't have coronaries. How are you doing?" She looked down and was surprised to see Thelma was also waiting on one number, B-3.

The caller cleared his throat and called out another number.

"B-3."

Compressed into the following two seconds, Margaret felt both monumental depression at having lost and elation at Thelma's good luck. She waited, but her friend was staring silently at her card. Margaret frowned and nudged Thelma.

"Bingo," someone else said.

"Thelma!" Margaret raised her voice and pointed.

"Oh my! Bingo!" Thelma called, but it came out too late and in a reedy voice that barely made it to the rostrum.

In another minute the game was all over. Chairs scraped back as people stood to return their cards, and good-natured grumbling mixed with goodbyes. Margaret just sat and stared at Thelma, as dumbfounded as if she had seen her friend burn her Social Security check.

Thelma started to cry. "I'm sorry, Margaret." Reaching into her sleeve and plucking out a handkerchief, she cried silently for another few moments while she dabbed at her eyes. After a minute she collected herself. "It's just too much."

"What is?"

"Everything." She blew her nose. "I can't take it anymore!" She broke into tears again.

Margaret put her arm around her friend. "What's bothering you, dear? Surely it can't be this little game. We always lose."

"I think—" Thelma stammered. "I think they want to kill me."

Two

     "I MOVED IN THERE FORTY-TWO YEARS ago,'' Thelma said over her steaming cup of tea. "I stayed on through both good and bad times, but it's always been my home. I'll be damned if they'll kick me out now.'' She and Margaret were sitting in Squire's Coffee Shop two blocks away from the church. It was an unusual stop for them after the bingo game but Margaret had insisted.

Normally, she would have been at home by this time, snuggled into her burgundy robe, fur slippers, and the heavy-meshed black hairnet she wore to bed. But Margaret could never resist the plight of a friend. Ever since the death of her husband, Oscar, she had stayed on in the West Eighty-first Street apartment, just off of Broadway, where they had lived happily together for many years. She kept herself going by becoming involved in the activities and problems of her neighborhood, even winning the grudging admiration of two police officers—David Schaeffer and Sam Morley—for some astute amateur sleuthing she had done in three murder cases. But Margaret was happiest in her daily routine. She would sit in the sun with her pigeon-loving friend, Bertie, or pin on one of her little hats and make her way to the Florence K. Bliss senior citizens' center. The evenings were reserved for the mystery stories she enjoyed and, occasionally, for an old-movie festival at the Thalia. For the moment it seemed this kind of peace was gone.

"Kick you out?'' Margaret repeated. She leaned forward

4

and peered kindly at the other woman. Thelma was in her early seventies, like Margaret, but would admit to no more than sixty-nine. Perhaps that explained the bright red hair. What it didn't explain was her 1950s-style full skirts that stopped three inches short of her ankles. Margaret didn't go in much for newfangled styles, but hemlines—that was something else.

"They want my apartment," Thelma said between sips. "Mine and Angelo's. We're the last two left."

Margaret ladled a spoonful of sugar into her tea and stirred it slowly. She waited for the spiraling liquid to settle, then lifted the cup.

"Who's they?"

Thelma shrugged. "I don't know. It's just a name—Mantex Management. They're the new agents who collect the rent. When I tried to call they weren't listed."

"But aren't you controlled or something? They can't just raise the rent willy-nilly."

"Oh, it's not the rent." Thelma shook her head. "See, the rest of the building is vacant now, all twenty-two apartments. Angelo Varonetti and I are the only ones that held out. Six floors with just the two of us rattling around. No, they want to tear the building down and that means it's gotta be totally empty." She looked around carefully then lowered her voice. "It wasn't clear at first, maybe two years ago. When the young ones moved out, Mantex just didn't rerent their apartments. Six months ago we were down to ten, all controlled, and then the awful things began."

Margaret lit her last cigarette and inhaled deeply. "What did they do?" she asked.

"What *didn't* they do? First it was noise. They let a rock band practice in the Bernsteins's old apartment on the third floor. Of course we complained, all of us, but by the time we finally got the police to impose the curfew, the Wilovs had left. 'Couldn't take it anymore,' Polly Wilov said. Ha, it was only the beginning." Thelma finished her tea and put the cup down with a clatter. Then she nervously twisted a strand of hair as she continued speaking. "A month later we all discovered, almost on the same day, that our apartments had become infested with cockroaches. I don't mean the odd bug here and there we had all come to expect. I mean we were overrun with them. I found three in my bed,'' she said with a shudder. "Someone had obviously imported several thousand and let them loose in the stairwells. That's when I tried calling Mantex, but their phone wasn't listed.''

"How awful," Margaret said.

"We called an exterminator. He sprayed the whole house, and the fumes were so terrible we had to vacate for the entire day. That evening we were stepping on dead bugs everywhere. We thought we'd won. But two days later a new batch showed up—I pulled two out of my hairbrush. That's when the Pearles decided it was time to move to Miami.'' Thelma let go of her curl of hair and made a fist. Margaret noticed for the first time that her knuckles looked slightly swollen from arthritis.

"Minna Pearle was my best friend. It makes me so mad.''

"I don't blame you. Couldn't you call the police again?''

"About cockroaches in New York! We didn't call the police again until they turned off the heat. That was sometime in January.''

"But that's illegal!''

"So it is," Thelma continued. "It was twenty-five degrees outside, and, after a few hours, forty-eight inside. Geraldo told us the boiler blew a fitting.'' She leaned forward. "He's the nasty handyman they send in one day each week—never has a nice word to say to anybody. Anyway, by the time the boiler got fixed, two weeks later, everyone had moved out but Angelo, Fran, and me. We were heating with the stoves and praying nothing would blow up. We held a meeting and decided to fight back. The junkies were hanging around the building like ants around honey. They got a sixth sense you know—can smell when a building is about to go under. After they strip it of all its metal, it's only a matter of time before the leaks make the floors collapse.''

"How'd you fight back?'' Margaret asked.

"Put padlocks on the doors of all the empty apartments

and a new lock on the front door. Then Angelo strung up lights in all the front rooms. He had to take power from the hall outlets because Con Ed had turned it off elsewhere. For a while we looked normal again, and the junkies went somewhere else. Then we hung a sheet from Angelo's living-room window that said 'Rent Strike,' as big as you please, and sat back to wait. That was the end of February." She smiled wryly. "By the end of April, Fran was gone."

"Gone?"

Thelma nodded. "She could put up with loud music, cockroaches, no heat, frozen pipes, and junkies on the stoop. She couldn't put up with the physical threats."

"Now this is too much!" Margaret said. "You don't mean to say someone hit her?"

"Oh no, nothing so crude." Thelma reached out and grabbed the waitress's apron as she was passing. "Warm up a slice of apple pie for me, honey. You want one, Margaret?" Margaret shook her head. She was too intent on listening to the rest of the story. Thelma closed her eyes and sat silently for a few long seconds.

"It started slowly—not only with Fran, with all of us. I'd be walking on a crowded street, and someone would bump into me. It's happened a hundred times before, but this time it was just a little different, a little more deliberate. The third time it happened the man actually knocked me over. He didn't stop to help me up, he just said if I didn't know how to walk on city streets I should move to the country."

"Very subtle."

"Exactly. Well, we were all very upset but what could we do? We went to the Office of Rent Control to complain, and they sent a letter off to Mantex. Far as I know they're still waiting for an answer. After the jostling they got rougher. Angelo was mugged on our block—his wallet was stolen, and he was pushed around. The mugger made it quite clear; said it was a dangerous block and that maybe Angelo shouldn't live there. This just made Angelo angry, but Fran got really scared. From then on she couldn't leave the house without Angelo or me. Of course, there was nothing we could do when they put a rock through her window.''

Margaret gasped just as the apple pie made an appearance. ''A rock?''

Thelma took a quick bite. ''Clear through her new carnival glass vase.'' Thelma leaned closer. ''Had this awful collection.''

''But by then, surely the police—''

''Too late. The next day the movers came, and we were down to two.'' She took another mouthful and shook her head. ''Fran had been there thirty-five years, almost as long as I have. It's a shame. She moved into a decrepit single-room hotel and comes by every day just to stare up at her old apartment.'' Thelma sighed. ''At least she's safe. No one's out after her anymore.''

''But Thelma, can't you make an agreement with them? Perhaps they'd be able to find you another apartment only a few blocks away and give you enough money to relocate.''

Her friend grinned. ''Yes, well, after Fran left, Mantex sent both Angelo and me notes. You wouldn't believe how nice they sounded. They'd be happy to offer us each five thousand dollars if we chose to vacate. What a joke! I'm paying a hundred and seventy-five dollars a month now. If I were to move, I couldn't find anything for under four hundred, so their offer wouldn't last me more than a year and a half. And then what!'' She stabbed the last bite of pie angrily. ''Well, Angelo is an old Sicilian. He's still got a lot of spirit.'' She chuckled, remembering something. Margaret waited.

''What did he do?'' she finally asked.

''He wrote just as polite a note back to them saying he appreciated their kind offer and that he'd be delighted to move for the sum of one hundred thousand dollars—cash.''

''One hundred thousand!''

''That's what I said to him, but he wouldn't budge. 'One hundred thousand or nothing,'. he insisted. Then he hung another sheet from his window—'Mantex is mauling me.' The place was getting to look like an overworked laundry. Boy, did it set them off. Two weeks later, there was an eviction notice on Angelo's door. That awful Geraldo let them in.''

"But eviction on what grounds?" Margaret asked. "Non-payment of rent?''

"No. Angelo had this little parakeet called Henry. Took care of him as if it was his son. He even trained him to pick sesame seeds off a Big Mac. Well, we all knew he had him, but no one paid it any mind. After all, other people had pets. The Wilovs had this awful cat that would slash your ankles as soon as roll over. But when we were down to the two of us, Mantex enforced the no-pet rule that was in our old leases.''

"Over Henry?''

Thelma nodded. "Over Henry!" There was silence for a moment. Margaret reached in her purse and came up with the empty cigarette pack. She looked at it disgustedly and dropped it by her cup. "Filthy habit. I should stop.''

"You and Angelo both," Thelma said. "He goes through a pack a day.''

"What about Henry?" Margaret asked. "Did Angelo have to get rid of him?''

Thelma nodded slowly. "It nearly killed him, but he let him go in Central Park. The little fella followed him on the way home, too. Got as far as Broadway then just disappeared. Next day Angelo packed all the rest of his bird seed, about four pounds of it, and mailed it to Mantex along with the eviction notice.''

"When was that?" Margaret asked.

"About a month ago.''

"And what's happened since then?''

Thelma frowned, and her hand smoothed back the loose strand of hair. She leaned closer and whispered. "Nothing.''

"Nothing?''

Thelma shook her head.

"So there's nothing to worry about. They've probably given up.''

"Never! They're planning something, I know it. They're too close to give in now. I'm going crazy." She ran a hand over her forehead. "But Margaret, I won't move. I've lived there too long."

Margaret patted her friend's arm. "Of course you won't move, dear. But I think you're letting it get the better of you. Missing that full-card bingo—" Margaret shook her head. "Come on, I'll walk you home." She looked at her watch. "It's very late." The two women paid and left the restaurant. A half-block away, Margaret spoke again. "Maybe I should talk to Sam Morley about it. There's a community relations meeting at the end of next week. He should know what terrible things happen to the older people in his precinct."

Thelma lifted her head. "Precinct?"

"The Eighty-first." Margaret smiled. "Lieutenant Morley and I have, shall we say, a working relationship. He always listens to me." The two women arrived at the corner of Columbus Avenue and waited for the light to change.

"It can't wait two weeks," Thelma said softly. "Something might happen tomorrow."

"Just stay calm," Margaret said. "People don't get killed for their apartments." The light was about to change, and as Margaret took Thelma's arm to cross the street, a last car sped up to make the crossing. Thelma stepped out into the street at the same moment that Margaret screamed.

"Watch out!" She pulled back on Thelma's arm and wrenched her a step back. As she did so, a thin silver object skimmed by with incredible speed only a foot away. It hit ten yards up the block and kept bouncing and rolling until it crashed into a trash can, knocking it over. A young woman who was also waiting to cross came over to help.

"Hubcap," she said shaking her head. "Those things can be lethal. Car must have hit a bump. Are you both all right?"

Thelma took a deep breath, watching the car speed downtown. Its back left wheel was without a cover. "Yes," she said. "Must have been a freak accident." But she looked at the smooth roadway and frowned at Margaret. Together they crossed the street, and when they were on the other side, Margaret bent close to Thelma and whispered, "I'll speak to Lieutenant Morley tomorrow."

Thelma stared at her friend. "You don't think . . . ?"
Margaret nodded. "I saw him throw it!"

Three

SERGEANT DAVID SCHAEFFER HAD THE
kind of awkward face photographers love. His nose was as
thin as a dime-store novel, and his two eyes looked as if they
were not quite on speaking terms with each other. There was
a white scar on his cheek where a ricochet from a .38 slug
had run through his beard like a clear cut for a power trans-
mission line. Had his face been an art-school design project,
the student would have failed. Yet his face was ideally suited
to his profession. Schaeffer was one of the Eighty-first Precinct's undercover cops and his haphazardly set features were
as much in keeping with his general appearance as were his
torn sneakers, his ripped jeans, and his single gold earring.
He smiled at Margaret with a grin that made up for the rest
of his face.

"Sam's just had a run-in with the budget office," he said.
"It's not the best time to drop by, unless of course you've
got several thousand dollars to donate to the cause."

"Humph, can't walk in the streets at night, never a cop
around, and you want more money. What for, uniforms?"

Schaeffer laughed. "No, patrolmen. Our roster was cut
back by a three-man shift."

"If this keeps up, I'm going to move to Miami. Is Sam in
his office?"

Schaeffer nodded. "I suppose you want me to tell him you're waiting."

"But I'm not," she said, marching to the door of Morley's office. She turned the knob and walked in.

Lieutenant Morley was hunched over a black loose-leaf notebook, intent on the column of figures before him. He was wearing a brown plaid shirt open at the collar. A spotted green tie was being squeezed to death between the edge of the desk and his belly. Without looking up he growled, "Yeah, what is it?"

"You always this polite?" Margaret said lightly and took her favorite seat, the brown Naugahyde armchair with the scar on one of its wooden arms. It was her favorite seat because it was right by Morley's ever-present pack of Camels.

Morley looked up at her impatiently. He took in her neat gray hair, the little hat perched above it, her open face, and lively eyes. "What do you think this is, a fruit stand? Can't you see I'm busy?" He leaned back and squinted at her through his reading glasses. If his fifty-three years had been kind to him, it didn't show on his face. Most of the hair on his head had retreated to the area above his ears. The lines on his forehead had more depth, but not nearly the symmetry of the lines at the corners of his mouth. Above all he looked tired. Except for the eyes, he had the face of a hotel janitor or maybe a corner man for a club boxer. But the eyes, when you got through the smudged glasses, were keen and monitory. The people who had misread their message were sorry that they hadn't been more observant. Most of those people were in prison. Margaret, from the very beginning, had understood.

"Fruit stand? No, unless you're pushing sour grapes." She winked. "Come on. It's not every day you see your most community-spirited senior citizen." Margaret reached for the pack of Camels.

"Yeah, so tell me, what am I going to say when some other senior citizen gets mugged on a street that used to be patrolled? We just lost a shift because the mayor wants to balance his goddamned budget."

"Schaeffer told me."

"Who ever heard of a balanced budget anyway?" Morley threw the pencil down, took off his glasses, and rubbed them with a dirty handkerchief from his back pocket. When he put them back on, Margaret saw the smudges had been wiped into a homogeneous film. "So, what are you doing here, Margaret? I only see you these days when you've got something on your mind."

"I do," Margaret sighed. She lit the cigarette she had just cadged and blew a cloud past Morley's left ear. "A friend of mine needs some help."

"Well, thank God it's not another murder. What kind of help? Your friend want to complain about the prices at Zabar's?"

Margaret crushed her cigarette out. "Sam, you have a perverse and patronizing sense of humor which is your least admirable trait. I don't like it one bit." She looked at him like a seventh-grade math teacher regarding her worst pupil. Within ten seconds Morley sat upright and mumbled an apology.

"Go ahead."

"My friend happens to be a seventy-two-year-old woman who is being harassed illegally and pressured into leaving her apartment. The owner wants to tear the building down and throw her onto the street."

"At her age she's probably protected."

"Against hubcaps thrown at her out of speeding cars?"

Morley sighed. "Okay, maybe you better tell me about it. If it were anybody else, I'd send them out to the desk sergeant." He looked up. "But you have a certain knack—"

"Her name is Thelma Winters," Margaret said, watching silently as he wrote the name down. Then she repeated the conversation she had had with Thelma, trying to remember as many of the details as possible. She finished with the close call they'd had on Columbus Avenue, then sat back and waited for Morley to say something. He was looking at the eraser of his pencil, and when he answered, Margaret was shocked.

"Before I tell you there's little I can do," he began, "let

me explain that this kind of harassment is as common as snatching gold chains on the subway. Don't think Thelma Winters's situation is unique."

"Yes," Margaret said, "but so is grand larceny a common situation, and the police don't turn their backs on that."

"Grand larceny is a crime," Morley said. "You tell me on what grounds you want me to go after Mantex."

"Attempted murder," Margaret said.

"Why? Because one of their tenants almost got hit by a loose hubcap? You should know how many hubcaps Sanitation finds on the streets every month. What crime's been committed?"

"Does that mean you have to wait until someone is seriously hurt before you take an interest?"

"No." Morley leaned back. "I suppose we could take preventative measures. We could station a patrolman outside the door twenty-four hours a day." He looked down at the budget report and sighed. "Except this isn't 1950, and I just lost three men whom I'll probably have to pull from the Broadway detail. I'm sure as hell not pulling another three to hang around a nearly empty building." He let that sink in. "What you really ought to do," Morley continued, "is have your friend go to the Enforcement Division of the Office of Rent Control, file a complaint with them, and they'll investigate. They're set up to deal with just this kind of case."

"She's already done that. It was about as effective as canned chicken soup. Nothing came of it."

Morley sighed and tried to loosen the spotted tie. "Well then, go to the Bureau of Housing and get them to send an inspector. If Mantex didn't provide heat in the winter, you could have nailed them on that. Maybe they are in violation of something else now. But it's the housing authorities you want, not the police."

Margaret was silent for a long minute. "So you won't help," she finally said. "I can't believe it. Thelma was almost killed—"

Morley looked pained. He thought of the help Margaret had given the Eighty-first Precinct, including the cookies she was always baking for them. "Listen, Margaret, I got about a half-dozen robberies and street muggings a night, about one hundred hookers that have to be dealt with, fifteen murders a year, four or five serious accidents a day, and you want me to play nursemaid to some old lady who's got real-estate problems. I'd like to help, really I would. I just don't have the people." He looked at her and shifted uncomfortably. Margaret just stared back at him coldly. After fifteen seconds she stood up.

"Where are you going?" he said.

"To get some fresh air and to see about helping a friend." Jabbing her hatpin into her hat with more force than usual, she strode out of the office without saying goodbye. Morley couldn't remember the last time he'd seen her so angry.

Four

"IT SEEMS TO ME," MARGARET SAID, "THE first thing we have to do is to find out who this Mantex is." She was seated on one of the benches on the Eighty-second pedestrian island in the middle of Broadway—a place she often visited. Next to her were Angelo Varonetti and Thelma. For a man in his seventies, Varonetti had a big frame, a friendly smile that reminded Margaret of Spencer Tracy, and a shock of white hair. Dressed in an old blue golf jacket and a pair of rumpled brown slacks, he was leaning forward on the bench toward them, a cigarette dangling from his mouth. A brown nicotine stain on his right index finger showed that there had been many other cigarettes in the past.

"Mantex," Angelo said, "is only a name. And Box 248, Elmira, New York, is the only thing I've been able to find out about them. That's as much as I get off my rent bills every month. They're not listed in the phone book; they're not members of any managing agents associations in New York; The Realty Advisory Board here, the people that handle all the union negotiations, don't have them listed; and the Chamber of Commerce in Elmira, New York, never heard of them." He shook his head. "A total blank and I'm sure it's not by accident." He took a drag on his cigarette and stamped it out on the pavement.

"But what about Geraldo?" Thelma said.

"Geraldo's a mean S.O.B. He wouldn't give his mother a dime for a cup of coffee."

"Forty-five cents," Margaret said lightly. "But go on."

"Anyway, he comes in only on Monday. The rest of the time he's the super of another building nearby."

"One of Mantex's buildings?" Margaret asked.

"No, I checked that. But when I asked Geraldo if Mantex has other buildings in New York, he told me to mind my own business."

"I think he was the one that put all the roaches in the stairwell," Thelma added.

Margaret thought for a moment. "Has he been the super long?"

"About the time Mantex started pushing people out. Before that we had Mr. Taroz." She turned to Angelo. "Now he was a real gentleman."

"Well, the first thing we can do is have a talk with this Geraldo," Margaret said. "He'll tell us who his boss at Mantex is."

"It won't do any good," Angelo said. "He'll clam up."

"We'll see," Margaret said. "But that's not all we can do. There are the municipal records to be checked, and then there's another angle. Do either of you remember seeing a truck delivering fuel oil to the building?" She raised a hand to forestall an objection by Angelo. "I mean when you were getting heat."

Angelo shrugged his shoulders. "I don't," he offered.

"Wait a minute," Thelma said. "I think I remember a green truck."

"Green," Margaret prompted. "Did it have any writing on it?"

There was silence for a few seconds while Thelma tried to remember.

"Red letters," she said finally.

"And the word, was it a long one or a short one?"

"McQuill," Thelma blurted out. "McQuill Oil."

"That's right," Angelo said. "Now I remember."

"Good." Margaret sat back. "Now all we need to do is find out where they send their bills. That Elmira box number must have been just for their tenants. Maybe their suppliers have another address."

"How are you going to find it?" Angelo asked.

"Follow me," she said. "There's a phone at Squire's Coffee Shop." She rummaged in her old handbag before standing up. "I'm afraid I'll need a quarter."

"My pleasure," Angelo said and lifted a quarter from one of the pockets of his thin wallet. "Never know when you'll need a quarter for a phone call." He smiled.

"Or a dime for a cup of coffee." Margaret winked and started walking in the direction of the restaurant.

"That's right, I'm the bookkeeper for Mantex, and we're checking our records," Margaret said into the phone. "The accounting firm of Aarons and Stevens is running a double-check and they've come up with a slight discrepancy." Margaret paused and looked up into the faces of Thelma and Angelo listening anxiously outside the phone booth. "A discrepancy of $208.30," Margaret added in a serious voice. "Please check your billing records. Yes, I'll wait." Margaret leaned forward and smiled. "She's checking." After a minute and a half, Margaret nodded into the receiver. "You're sure, it's all paid in full? That's fine." She hesitated. "Now, I wonder if you could send us a confirming letter to that effect, for the people at Aarons and Stevens. Thank you.

You know where to send it." She held her breath. "Yes, it's the same place as in the billing address. That's right." Margaret looked again at her two friends. "That's it, thank you." She put the receiver back softly. It was a minute before she said anything.

"Well, they're certainly thorough. Box 248, Elmira, New York."

"I told you," Angelo said. "They don't want anyone to know who they are."

"Well," Margaret shrugged. "Strike one. We'd better get to work on those other possibilities. Let's go downtown right now. Besides, I won't be able to see Sidney until later this afternoon at the OTB."

"Who is Sidney?" Angelo asked.

"Oh, just an old friend," Margaret answered. "And the best person I know to talk to Geraldo."

Five

FOR THE ENTIRE RIDE DOWNTOWN, Thelma had a lock hold on Margaret's arm.

"I hate subways," Thelma said apologetically as they exited. "Make me nervous. You never know what's going to jump out at you—haven't taken one since VJ day."

Margaret was shocked. "I'd be lost without them," she said. She looked at Angelo, who seemed almost as relieved as Thelma to be back in the sunlight. "Besides, you meet so many interesting people down there—that's how I met Rose." Margaret chuckled. "She was struggling with her eight shopping bags and didn't see the empty bottle. I helped her up, fetched her things, and we started talking. Been friends ever since.''

"What was she doing with eight bags?" Thelma asked.

"Well," Margaret shrugged. "She's a bag lady."

There was an awkward moment of silence as they continued to walk. "Here we are," Margaret finally said, pointing to the large Municipal Building ahead of them. Now, let's stay together. If you got lost in there, you'd be gone for a week.''

They turned in and found themselves facing a big lobby. A lot of people were scurrying to and fro, but no one was at the information booth.

"Maybe the candy man will help us," Angelo suggested, walking over to the newsstand. After a minute he came back with a pack of cigarettes in his hand.

"Finance Administration, Real Property Assessment on nine. And, in case you're interested, Truant Baby in the seventh at Belmont. He was a regular mine of information." They headed for the elevators.

"Truant Baby, huh," Margaret said. The doors opened and they got in. Angelo pushed nine.

"Now what we've got to do first is see who's paying the taxes and where the tax bill is sent to," Margaret said. "It's very simple, you'll see."

They found the door to the tax department and pushed inside. In front of them was a big room with a long counter, on top of which were maybe thirty large books of computer printouts. There were five clerks sitting at desks behind the counter, and three of them were discussing Gooden's pitching performance of the previous night. Margaret cleared her throat.

"Excuse me," she began. One of the clerks looked up. She was a middle-aged black woman wearing horn-rimmed glasses and what looked like a size sixteen dress. Both the glasses and the dress appeared to be too small for her.

"I'd like to find out who owns the building at 621 West Ninety-first Street."

The large woman stood up and came over.

"You got a block and lot number?"

Margaret shook her head. "No."

"Just a minute." She disappeared behind a pillar and rustled some papers in another book. Then she reappeared and spouted off a number. "Over there," she pointed. "Fifth book from the end."

Margaret and her two friends walked over and started leafing through. It wasn't long before they came across the address they were looking for.

"So?" Thelma asked, looking past Margaret's shoulder.

"I don't understand," Margaret said, frowning. "It says that the tax is being paid by Fiben and Larson, and it gives an address in Newark. The owner is a firm called Santos Corporation, there's no address. Mantex isn't even listed." She looked up. "Who's Fiben and Larson?"

The clerk had walked over and now leaned lazily across the counter. She sighed heavily.

"Sounds like a law firm." The clerk raised herself up. "There are three types of parties listed here as taxpayers: owners, mortgagers like banks, and attorneys. More often than not, when it's an attorney it's because the real owner doesn't want to be known." She smiled. "You know, lawyer-client privileges and all that."

She looked at Margaret. "If you want to find out what this Santos Corporation is, you'll have to go over to the Surrogate's Court at Thirty-one Chambers. City Register's there. They'll be able to show you the deed, mortgage agreement, all that. You should be able to lift an address somewhere."

Margaret looked around at her two friends. "Strike two."

Thirty-one Chambers Street had enough marble in its baroque, double stair-cased central lobby to pave a mile of lower Broadway. It was a building too ornate for mere municipal offices. Choirs should have been chanting from the marble balcony while a 110-piece symphony orchestra filled its central space with music. As it was, Mortgage Filing Records was in room 205 and Microfilm was in room 202.

The three friends struggled up the wide rose-and-amber marble staircase in silence, hesitating at the door to Microfilm. There were no sounds coming through the heavy wooden arched doorway.

"Go ahead," Angelo prompted and turned the knob.

Margaret was the first one through. It was like jumping from the eighteenth century into the twenty-first. Microfilm readers, twenty-one in all, stood in three rows. A huge console file the size of a small lunch counter stood against one wall. Another, even larger, was in the center of the room. Several clerks were plucking transparent envelopes from numbered slots. There were a few desks on their right but only one was occupied. A young woman with a frizzy haircut and a striped black-and-white tee shirt was sorting through some papers. When she saw them and stood up, Margaret noticed her tight black pants. She walked the few steps over.

"Block and lot number please," she said before Margaret had a chance to open her mouth.

"I'm afraid I don't know how to operate the machines," Margaret said apologetically.

"You got a block and lot number?" the girl said. "I'll show you the machines."

"Wait a minute," Thelma said. "I wrote it down." She reached for a scrap of paper in her purse and read off a number.

"The third machine," the girl pointed. "I'll get the jacket."

After a few minutes, Thelma, Margaret, and Angelo were sitting in a tight semicircle behind the clerk at the microfilm reader.

"Everything after 1968 is in here," she said. "If the deed hasn't changed hands since then, you'll find it in the next room in those dusty books."

"No," Angelo said. "The building was sold about two and a half years ago."

The clerk started moving the controls. "What was the address again?"

"Six hundred twenty-one West Ninety-first Street."

In a few seconds she had it. The three pressed closer.

"Sold September 21, 1983, for six hundred fifty thousand dollars. Here's the deed. Party of the first part," she looked up, "that's the old owner, Siegel Corporation."

"That's right," Thelma exclaimed. "Old Mr. Siegel used to live in the building."

"But six hundred fifty thousand dollars," Angelo whistled. "For that old dump?"

"Who's the new owner?" Margaret interrupted.

The clerk moved her finger. "Party of the second part—Santos Corporation."

"And an address?" Margaret asked.

"Sure. Care of Bank Amalie, Grand Cayman, Bahamas."

"Bahamas?" Margaret repeated, staring at the girl. "What's a corporation down there doing buying a building on the Upper West Side?"

The clerk with the tight pants looked up.

"You kidding? Owner's probably having an egg cream right now on Canal Street. These offshore Bahamian corporations are so's you can't trace the owners. Makes it hard on the IRS." She unwrapped a stick of gum and slid it in her mouth. "Anything else you want?"

"Isn't there any place I could get an address here?" Margaret asked in exasperation.

The clerk frowned. "Maybe the mortgage agreement. There's the notary affidavit." She turned the dials more slowly as black page after page ran past the microfilm screen. "Wait a minute," she said and turned back a page. "Here it is. The mortgagor is a company called Financial Diversified Industries, located in Carmel, California," the clerk said. "At least they have a street address." Margaret wrote it down. "Mortgage is for five hundred thousand dollars at ten percent for three years. Dated the same as the deed, September 21." The woman continued. "Then it says that at option of mortgagor the mortgage can be increased to $2 million and converted to Mayberry Mews Development, Inc., for twenty-five years at the then current prime rate, application of paragraph twelve to be effective."

"What's paragraph twelve?" Margaret asked.

Shifting her gum, the clerk scanned the page then back-tracked. Two pages earlier in the mortgage instrument she found paragraph 12. It was only two sentences long:

In the event mortgage is converted to Mayberry Mews Development, Inc., mortgagor will participate with 15 percent equity in the mortgagee's development plan to be known as "Mayberry Mews." Prior to renewal corresponding documents will be drawn to effect such agreement and will be signed concurrently with new Mortgage.

"What's it mean?" Thelma said.

"I don't know." The clerk looked puzzled. "Let's see—" She ran the machine forward again. "Yes, here's the notary affidavit. We should be able to get an address for whoever signed the deed for Santos." She pointed to the seal and the notary's signature, one Benjamin Kamen, registration number 63 4782153. Above his seal it said, "on September 21, 1983, before me personally came Mr. Jason Moore, to me known, who, being duly sworn did depose and say that he resides at 725 East Eighty-fourth Street, New York City, and is the president of the Santos Corporation mentioned in the foregoing instrument—"

"Well," Margaret said, "finally we got something." She raised her pencil.

"No you don't," the clerk with the tight pants said. "The highest number before the river in the Eighties is under seven hundred." She gave Margaret a thin smile. "My boyfriend lives on Eighty-first Street. These notaries sometimes don't look too closely at supporting documents. After all, they make only fifty cents each affidavit."

"Damn!" Angelo said.

"Well, there's that Financial whatever company," Thelma said hopefully.

"Don't count on it," Margaret replied. "It could be just another blind alley." She looked around at her two friends.

"Besides, who's going to go out to California to find out? It could be an expensive wild-goose chase."

"Well," the clerk said. "That's about all you'll get from this." She started removing the microfilm jacket. "Of course, there are other agencies you can go to. Maybe they have some other information on this Santos Corporation."

"What other agencies?" Margaret asked without much enthusiasm.

"Bureau of Housing Violations. They're at Thirty-nine Broadway. Maybe there are some citations against the building with correspondence. Then there's the Department of Buildings, Office of Code Enforcement—all apartment buildings have to be registered with them every three years— also the Rent Control Agency at Two Lafayette Street." She pulled the plastic envelope out of the reader and turned the machine off. "Somewhere you'll probably find a bona fide address. I'm afraid that's all I can do for you here."

"Thank you," Margaret said, standing up. She turned to her two friends. "Looks like we have a long way to go."

"Strike three," Angelo said. "Next batter!"

Six

BY 3:55 THAT AFTERNOON THE NINETY-first Street OTB parlor was full of smoke and dejected bettors. It was not a good day for long shots and $2.80 payouts made for a lot of grumbling. Most of the people inside were men, but there were enough women around for Margaret to feel comfortable. Losing tickets littered the floor along with hundreds of crushed cigarettes, profile sheets, and used pages from *The Racing Form*. Margaret looked around quickly for her friend Sidney. There was no doubt he was there. Margaret couldn't remember the last time he had missed a weekday afternoon. She squinted to relieve her eyes from the smoke and checked the people in line at the windows. Her gaze traveled from one to another until it stopped on the short, plaid-jacketed man with the white mustache. She grinned and walked the few steps over to him.

"Truant Baby in the seventh," she whispered. "Bet the farm."

"Who says so?" the man muttered without so much as raising his eyes from his calculations.

"A man in an important government office. Trust me. How many tips I've given you have gone wrong?"

Sidney finally turned and smiled. "Margaret, you've never given me a tip, and this nag is at twenty to one."

She shrugged. "Suit yourself. Anyway, we've got to talk."

He looked at her closely. "If I bet two dollars on Truant Baby, it's a coffee if he loses."

Margaret smiled. "And if he wins?"

"I'll buy you twenty cups."

"Deal," Margaret said and watched as Sid turned and purchased a ticket. In a minute he was by her side.

"What's so important you gotta grab me in here? If I didn't know any better, I'd say you were acting just like a wife."

"Oh tosh!" Margaret reddened. "Not once did I ever interrupt Oscar's Wednesday-night poker games. This is the only place I can be sure to get you." She looked at his face creased with his seventy-four years but alive with the grin of a twenty-year-old. Of all her friends, Sidney was still the youngest at heart; a man who would admit his age proudly to watch the results from younger men. He still played handball at the YMCA twice a week and walked three miles a day to keep his "circulation hopping." In his youth he'd been a minor-league ball player, then, for many years, a clerk in a hardware store until he ended up selling piece goods for a firm in the West Thirties. He'd been retired for the last nine years, four of them as a widower. After Emma, whom he still talked about, the horses were his great love.

"I need your help," Margaret said. "But it's a big favor." She looked around. "We can't talk here."

Sidney held up his hand. "Not before I win my coffee." He looked at his watch. "The race will be on in a minute." There was still a lot of commotion in the office, even when a few seconds later the speaker on a wall console started calling out the seventh race. It was hard for Margaret to follow. Horses' names flashed out along with distance markers and times. At one point she heard that Truant Baby was on the outside and moving into fifth. A few seconds later, the horse was in second and driving for the finish line. Sid had his fist closed around the ticket and was making piston-like motions with his arm. Before Margaret could stop herself her hat was askew, and she was shouting, "Come on, Truant Baby!!" Suddenly the room quieted for the order of finish and then Sid threw his arms around Margaret.

"We won. Son-of-a-bitch—how do you like that!"

Margaret laughed, then leaned forward. "How much?" she whispered.

After two minutes of staring at the tote board, the numbers finally appeared. "Forty-two dollars and fifty cents! Christ, let me collect it." Margaret made a quick calculation. When he came back she had a grin on her face. "I'm hungry. How about trading in my twenty cups of coffee for a light meal."

"Sure. Where to?"

"Come on. You're in for a real treat. For once in your life, Sid Rossman, you're going to eat something other than bagels, brisket, or bananas in cream."

Sid groaned. "Not again. The last time it was some awful barbeque that was burned to a crisp."

She grabbed his arm and they headed out of the OTB office.

"You won't have that problem this time." She smiled. "We're going Japanese."

Seven

"BIT EARLY FOR FOOD," SID SAID AS THEY sat down at the table at Hisae's. He was already eying the little slabs of uncooked fish nearby with great skepticism.

"Having second thoughts?" Margaret smiled weakly. The walk to the restaurant had just about done her in. "I'll have a Jack Daniels on the rocks," she added without hesitation. "Hold the twist." She leaned back and closed her eyes.

Sid watched her carefully. The waiter came over and took the drink orders. Sid wanted a beer. It was another minute before Margaret spoke.

"Don't ever let me go below Seventy-second Street again."

"Would you mind telling me what this is all about?"

Margaret sat forward. "Eight government offices, eight different locations, eight sets of records, eight clerks trying to be helpful, and zero," she held up her fingers to show him, "zero information. I couldn't believe it."

The waiter came back with Margaret's drink and Sid's Budweiser. He stood waiting for the order.

"I'll have some tekka maki, yellow fin tuna, sea urchin, and an eel roll," Margaret said, pointing. "How about you, Sid? If you've never had it before you might like to try some fluke."

"If I do it will be," he said. "No, I'll stick with my beer. I'm not really hungry." He gave the sushi on display another look and took a big gulp of Budweiser. "So, what were you looking for?"

Margaret drank some of the Jack Daniels and peered into the glass. The liquor warmed her body and relaxed her.

"I'm sorry, Sid, I guess I should start at the beginning." She smiled, then sat back. "It all began when Thelma missed a big bingo pot." She took another slow sip from her drink and continued for ten minutes with her story.

"You mean to say you can't find out who owns that building?" Sid asked. His eyes had narrowed and he was leaning over his second beer.

"Not even the Motor Vehicles Bureau has any outstanding parking tickets on Jason Moore. That's how far I went. For all I know it's an alias. I need another approach. Official channels don't work."

"So you thought of old Sidney." He laughed. "I can't imagine why. Nothing I can do—not after what you've told me."

"Oh yes there is," Margaret said. "You're just the man I need." She was about to explain when the waiter came back. Margaret raised her empty glass. "To Truant Baby." She watched as the waiter put her plate down. Sidney looked at it and winced. "There's only one problem," she continued. "The badge I got for you is not too authentic."

Sid had his glass halfway to his mouth. It hung in midair as he asked, "What in hell do I need a badge for?"

"All city building inspectors have badges. I saw one when I went to the Buildings Department. They're little gold and blue things." She smiled and stabbed a little rice ball with a piece of white fish on it wrapped in seaweed. "There's no way we can pass you off as a building inspector without one."

Sid exploded. "What are you talking about? That's fraud."

"Whatever." Margaret waved Sid's objection away. "What Mantex or Santos or God-knows-whoever is doing to Angelo and Thelma is worse." She popped the sushi in her mouth and started in on another. After a minute she pointed at him with the fork. "You're the only person I know who could impersonate a building inspector and get away with it.

You spent over thirty years in the hardware business, didn't you? You know plumbing, you know electrical. Throw a few catchy terms around and you'll get by.''

"What about the badge?"

Margaret reached into her purse again and flipped a gold-colored piece of metal on the table. Sid leaned forward.

"What's this, 'Tooney Town Police Department'?"

"Closest I could get at the toy store. It's the same shape and size. Maybe if we use a little blue paint—"

"Are you crazy? I'd be spotted in a minute."

"Not if you're quick and talk a good line—"

"Just a moment," Sid said and put down his glass. "You're asking me to stick my neck out using a piece of tin junk like that. Not on your life!"

"But Sid—"

"No 'buts.' Least we can do is get a decent shield, one with a New York City seal." A little grin appeared on his face. "And I just happen to know a guy who's got one. He's a retired elevator inspector. He once told me his shield, his pension, and two crushed fingers are the only things he took away after forty years on the job. We've warmed many a bar stool together in the last five years. I think he'd let me borrow it for an afternoon." He pushed the toy shield back across the table to Margaret. "Better than this piece of junk anyway."

Margaret beamed. "I'm sure there's an elevator in their building. That solves so many problems. Probably hasn't been looked at in years."

Sid finished his beer and put the glass to one side. He looked momentarily at the rest of the sushi on display, then back at the empty bottle and finally made a decision. He raised his hand to call the waiter over. "I'll have some of that," he said. "The little white stuff. Make sure there's plenty of rice." There was a moment of silence as the waiter wrote it down. "So," he said after he left. "Now for the big question. Why the hell do you want me to be an elevator inspector?"

"I told you—I need to find out who owns the building."

"And how am I supposed to do that?"

"Easy," Margaret said. She flashed a smile that any side-show carny would have been proud of. "You've never heard of greasing the wheels of capitalism?"

Sid looked blank.

"Graft," she said in a conspiratorial whisper. "We're going to apply some pressure and see what happens." She leaned back when the new plate arrived. "That was very brave of you, Sid. Even I've never had the squid."

Eight

THE WEATHER WAS DISMAL ON MONDAY. A mid-summer low-pressure front brought heavy rain and blustery winds. Sid wrapped an old trench coat over a plaid shirt and jeans and grabbed a battered felt hat to keep the water from running down his neck. This was one of the thirty times a year he asked himself why he lived in New York. The answers always came with the same unassailable logic: his rent-controlled apartment, his friends, and his rituals like the breakfast bagels at the Greek coffee shop. It still didn't make him feel any better when he had to face weather more suited to an Atlantic oil rig than to a cozy retirement village. He checked his mailbox in the lobby on the way out but it was still too early. The mail never arrived before 11:30, and now they were talking about mail deliveries only four times a week. Sid shut the little door angrily. Everywhere the same thing, service getting worse and costs going up. He could still remember when there were two deliveries a day and the first one at nine o'clock in the morning. "It's probably no better in Florida," he muttered, and trudged out into the rain.

Ten minutes later he was in front of the building. Angelo's "Mantex is Mauling Me" sign hung limply in the rain, its message partly obscured by the folds in the sheet. A light was on in the window next to it as well as another light two floors below. All the other windows were slate gray reflecting the cloud-rumpled sky. Sidney took a breath, fingered his borrowed elevator inspector's shield, and started up the stairs. He noticed that the lock had been left open as arranged by Margaret. He pushed the door open and entered. A chalky, damp, plaster smell hung in the air and made him hesitate. The entrance foyer was dim, the only light coming from a small, twenty-five-watt bulb overhead. He could barely make out the wallpaper pattern. In spots the paper was lifting away from the wall and curled in at the edges. Walking carefully over to the small, self-service elevator, Sid pushed the button, heard the electric motor start up and then cough once as the car descended. Ten seconds later, it was opening its door at the main floor. Sid got in, turned around, and found the basement button in a welter of Magic Marker graffiti. The doors started closing but stopped with an inch of airspace left. He waited another ten seconds and pressed the "door close" button but still nothing happened. Finally, he pressed the inner door together with his hands until the two sides made contact. The car bumped into gear and descended to the basement. When the door opened, Sid found himself looking at a short, stocky man with a dark, pugnacious face and a dirty tee shirt. He had a wrench in his left hand.

"Yeah, what do you want?"

"You the super?" Sid asked quickly.

"Who wants to know?" The man's eyes seemed to contract under dark bushy eyebrows. "And how'd you get in?"

"Name's Heller." Sid flashed the little badge attached to a leather card case he'd borrowed. "Elevator inspector—the door was unlocked."

Geraldo scowled and looked at the badge. "Christ, more

bullshit. We only got two people living here—one on the first floor. Why don't you go somewhere else that can use you.''

"I think," Sid said, motioning to the malfunctioning door, "you can use me." He stepped out of the car. "Your last inspection was over two years ago. About time you had another.''

The man stared at Sid for a long moment not saying anything. Finally he mumbled, "Go ahead, just don't bug me.''

"Where'll you be if I need you?"

Geraldo looked at his watch. "I got another hour here. After that you're on your own. I gotta go to 573 West Ninety-first and do some work there.''

Sid took a flashlight from his raincoat pocket and then hung the coat and hat on a nail. In his back pocket he had an adjustable wrench and a Phillips screwdriver. A big ring of old keys dangled from his belt loop.

"Hey, Pop, ain't you kinda old to be doing this?"

"Retiring next year," Sid said. "But don't worry. I still climb around pretty good." He got back into the elevator and found the standard door bypass switch his friend had told him about on the frame. Then he moved the car up a few feet and pressed the emergency stop. Easing himself down to the concrete floor and standing next to Geraldo, he took out his flashlight and shot it into the pit of the elevator shaft. "I'll start down there with the motor. Work my way up. I'll let you know." Geraldo watched for a few moments as Sid climbed down into the well five feet below the level of the basement.

When Geraldo had moved away, Sid found a fresh cigar in his pocket, lit it, and looked around at the airless, trash-strewn pit. The flare of the match briefly illuminated the damp, scarred walls, then died out. Without thinking of what lay under the trash, Sid worked his way over to the motor and flashed his beam on it. He forced himself to stay down for at least five minutes. Most of that time he bent over the motor, nervously smoking his cigar. Then he climbed back out, brought a chair over, and stepped up into the car. Releasing the basement door bypass, he brought the car all the way up to the top floor. Only then did he release his vise-like grip on the stogie and slump to the floor. He looked at his watch and made note of the time. He'd have to kill a half hour. "Then," he grimaced, "comes the hard part."

Geraldo was bent over a pipe on the floor when Sid came down to the basement thirty minutes later. The superintendent heard him coming and stood up. The wrench was locked around the bolts of a saddle-fitting connection. Geraldo wiped putty off his hands and waited for Sid to speak.

"You got problems," Sid began, shaking his head. "The bx cable connection on the motor is crushed and needs to be replaced before she shorts out. The bearings need relining on the main cable pulley, and that door track needs to be replaced. If it was only one thing I could give you a warning with a grace period, but with all three—" Sid shook his head. "I gotta close you down."

Geraldo frowned. "Hey, I don't know anything about that. This elevator's been going good since I got here."

"You call that good?" Sid raised his voice. "You get a short in the motor, and you can strand someone overnight in the car. Same thing with the pulley, it can lock up on you anytime. I don't care how many tenants you got, you got visitors, deliveries—you can't take the chance." Sid walked over and pulled a pen and a small notebook out of his raincoat pocket. "You won't be able to operate the elevator until these things are taken care of."

Geraldo shrugged. "So, the guy on the third floor walks." A little grin came over his face. "Tell you the truth, I don't think my boss is gonna give a damn about you closing it down. You might be doing him a favor."

"Yeah, well listen," Sid said, sticking the half-smoked cigar back in his mouth. "You tell your boss that this department's got a memory. Law says once he's got an elevator he's got to maintain it properly or take it out completely and brick up the shaft. That means the pulleys, weights, cables, and car. Runs into a lot of money. If he doesn't comply we can get very rough on him, and that means any other buildings he's got, or even this one if he's planning a J51 conversion.'' Sid spun the wheel on his old Zippo lighter. ''So I think maybe you should take this more seriously. I'm not out here climbing around for my goddamn health.'' He pointed at the fitting Geraldo had been working on. ''Not to mention that we got friends in the plumbing inspectors' division who might not like that jury-rigged connection. You know saddles are not supposed to be used for waste lines.'' Sid frowned as he relit the cigar. ''So maybe you should listen.''

Geraldo looked down at his connection, then back at Sid. ''This is an old building,'' he said defensively.

''Yeah, and I'm an old inspector. That doesn't necessarily mean I skirt the law. . .'' There was a silence while Sid wrote something in his notebook. ''. . . without good reason,'' he added slowly, still looking at his book.

Geraldo cleared his throat. A glint of understanding further hardened his face.

''What's that mean?''

Sid raised his eyes. ''Means I'm retiring next year. Take it from there.''

Geraldo chuckled. ''Hell, you guys are all alike. Come in here spouting codes and infractions and leave with a full wallet—bunch of grafters.''

''Hey,'' Sid pointed. ''I'll leave right now, and you'll get your citation tomorrow morning. If my guess is correct you'll also get your ass nailed by your boss.''

Geraldo's face still held the smirk. ''How much?'' Sid shrugged. ''Two bills. The repairs will cost you close to two grand.'' He put his pen back in his pocket. ''Cash.''

''You think I got that kind of dough here? You're crazy.''

''No,'' Sid smiled. ''I think you got a telephone here— I'm patient.''

''Not in this dump. The phone's over at 573, the same phone I could use to turn you in,'' Geraldo said evenly. ''You wouldn't have to wait a year to retire.''

''That would be real stupid—no evidence, no corroboration. You'd just be asking for a lifetime of failed inspections.''

Neither of the two men moved. Sid was beginning to

perspire even though it was chilly in the basement. After a minute, he shook the remaining drops of water off his hat and placed it back on his head.

"What's it going to be?" Sid asked.

"Come on, ain't my money. And it ain't the first time either." He brushed past Sid and got in the elevator. "Just pisses me off, that's all."

"Well, don't let it get to you." Sid smiled and followed Geraldo up to the rain-slick pavement and then on to the other building, a block away.

Unlike Angelo's and Thelma's building, 573 West Ninety-first had plenty of life in it yet; but the tenants looked out through windows coated with grime, sills that were warping, and masonry that was chipped. An odor of garlic and stale beer wafted to the bottom of the front stoop. On the first floor, right next to the entrance, a pair of dirty red mesh curtains helped complete the impression of a bloodshot and vaporous old structure. Geraldo walked in without saying anything to the several children playing on the stoop. A minute later Sid and the super were in the basement in a tiny office. An old wooden swivel-back chair with a dusty cushion was pushed in front of a scarred formica desk. Tools cluttered the floor in no discernible pattern, and the walls had several nude pinups and a pipe company calender. A single fluorescent bulb lit up the confined space with a flat light that merged everything. Geraldo sat down heavily and pulled a black telephone closer to him on the desk. Looking around, Sid saw no other chairs, so he stood with his back to the wall and relit his cigar. The walk had done little to calm his nerves. Geraldo stared at Sid over his shoulder, then turned and searched the desk top. There were several telephone numbers haphazardly inked into its white scratched surface. His finger traced from one to another until it came to rest on one with a line under it. Sid moved closer to the desk as Geraldo dialed.

"Damn my eyes," Sid whispered beneath the dialing sound. The number was still a blur, and he was as close as he could get without leaning on Geraldo's shoulder. If he got the number, he could forget about the rest of Margaret's crazy plan. The probability of Geraldo's boss turning down the bribe was too great, and if he went for it, following Geraldo to the pickup was risky at best. The telephone number was the key. Sid squinted but still the digits remained out of focus.

"Mr. M, it's Geraldo. I got a problem here." Geraldo swiveled around and faced Sid. He looked up at him closely. "I got an elevator inspector here looking for some money. Son-of-a-bitch wants two hundred dollars or he says he's going to make trouble." There was silence in the room as Geraldo listened to the man on the other end of the phone. "That's what I told him but he said they'd get rough in the future—you know, for a conversion or something." Geraldo listened again and his face broke out in a broad grin. "Yeah, sure," he said into the receiver and hung up. The grin stayed on his face as he pushed the phone away.

"The owner of the building says 'shove it,' " Geraldo said with pleasure. "Take your bribe and go elsewhere." His eyes narrowed. "Now beat it!"

Sid tried again to see the number on the desk and then made a quick decision.

"Just wait and see what happens. You're going to need a turnstile to let in all the inspectors." Sid raised his voice and felt his face getting flushed. "There's enough violations in that building to keep your man in the courts for years. The elevator is only the beginning—you've got plumbing, electrical, boiler—"

"Out!" Geraldo shouted, moving toward Sid.

"—And don't say I didn't give you the chance. You and your stupid boss blew it," Sid finished, turning to go. As he did so, he puffed on his cigar then took it out of his mouth and threw it away disgustedly. As bad as Sid's eyes were, he could see the pile of oily rags next to the wall. The lit cigar landed in the middle of the rags instantly causing a puff of fire.

"Son-of-a-bitch," Geraldo shouted, running to the burning pile. Sid turned around with a look of surprise. The super tried stamping out the flames, but the oil got on his shoe and the fire licked around his foot. Cursing again, he lunged quickly for a small fire extinguisher next to the door. Sid moved out of his way, stepping toward the desk. A blast of foam snuffed out the fire on Geraldo's boot, and three seconds later did the same to the pile of rags. An acrid cloud of smoke hung a foot down from the ceiling, but the whole episode was over in twenty seconds.

"I should knock your head off," Geraldo yelled.

Sid held his hands up. "I'm going, I'm going." He moved back toward the door. "Sorry if I was careless." He hurried through the door and out of the building. Sid was over two blocks away before he let the tiniest smile cross his face.

Nine

"EIGHT-SEVEN-THREE-SEVEN-THREE-FIVE-one?" Margaret asked. "You're sure?" She wrote the number down on a scrap of paper and studied it. Afternoon sunlight flecked her book-filled tables, a pigeon cooed on the windowsill, and coffee steamed in front of a plate of freshly baked cookies. Margaret was sitting in her easy chair and Sid's triumph over Geraldo glowed in his face.

Leaning over the table next to her, she brought a New York phone book onto her lap, opened it to the Moores, and started tracing down the columns. It was slow work. There were seven columns of listings, and more than once she looked up and rubbed her eyes before continuing. After ten minutes she shook her head slowly.

"Not here. That's funny."

"Maybe with only one 'o,' or without the 'e,' " Sid suggested.

"Tried it."

"Maybe another borough."

"Doubtful," Margaret added. "I recognize the 873 exchange as being for the Upper West Side. It's the old Trafalger three."

"Yeah," Sid said. "Emma's sister on West Eighty-sixth Street used to be a TR3."

Margaret got up and began to walk, making the pigeon wheel away. After a minute she stopped and faced Sid.

"There's nothing left to do but to call direct. The information operator won't give out an address from just a telephone number."

"Call? With what?" Sid asked. "Tell him someone's bought him a pizza and by the way what's his address?" Sid shook his head and stared at Oscar's photograph.

"Let me think." Margaret lit a Camel. "We're almost there." She exhaled a cloud of smoke and watched as it swirled with the room's air currents. Sid saw her lips form silent sentences—Margaret's way of testing ideas. She closed her eyes often and hardly noticed when she dropped a one-inch ash on her good Persian prayer rug. Finishing her cigarette, she was halfway through another before she reached for the phone.

"What are you going to do?" Sid asked.

"Listen." She looked at her watch and noted that it was still business hours. Then she dialed the number and sat back in the couch. After three rings the phone was answered. A man with a voice as oily as seaweed said, "Yes?"

"This is the telephone business office calling." Margaret tried to sound as official as possible. "As a last courtesy, we're calling to notify you that your telephone will be disconnected tomorrow at midnight unless we receive your payment of $145.62 by 5:00 P.M. I'm sorry we're forced to terminate service, but you haven't answered our last three warning notices."

"Hold on, lady," the voice said. "You must be mistaken. All our bills are paid."

"I'm sorry," Margaret said. "By 5:00 P.M."

"Wait!" The man shouted, all traces of civility gone. "You can't turn this phone off. I have the check stubs."

"Is this 873-7351?" Margaret asked. There was silence for a second.

"Yeah." The man on the other end of the phone sounded puzzled.

"And you are Mr. Thomas James, 282 West Sixty-fifth Street?"

"No, I'm not Thomas James." His voice rose with anger.

"You're not? But that's strange. Mr. James's phone number is listed on my terminal as 873-7351. I don't understand."

"Listen, lady, check your goddamn records again. Goose your computer or something. My name's not James—it's Farrell, and I've had this phone for the last ten years. You cut off my service and I'll sue you bastards."

Margaret winced as she heard the other phone slam onto the cradle. She laid her own down gently, then she quickly turned the pages of the phone book until she had it.

"Jason Farrell, 238 Central Park West, 873-7351."

She smiled at Sid. "Mantex Management."

Ten

SCHAEFFER WAS WEARING ONE OF HIS familiar disguises, that of a wino, when Margaret found him the next morning. Sprawled on a bench facing the river with the "Home" section of the *Times* draped over his face, he was watching a couple of lads jiving down a nearby path. Margaret unceremoniously pulled away the paper and asked him to sit up.

"Hey, you're blowing my cover," Schaeffer grumbled.

Margaret placed a brown paper bag in his lap.

"I got you some coffee. Jacobson told me where to find you. Forget this petty larceny stuff, I need you."

"So do the muggees of the city."

"At nine o'clock?"

Schaeffer took the lid off the container and inhaled the steam from the hot coffee.

"Yeah, I guess you're right. At this hour any self-respecting mugger is still in bed. Now, you take those two," he pointed. "Just because I busted the taller one last month doesn't mean he's not going to try another stickup." He smiled sarcastically and took a sip of the light-brown liquid. "Had to spend all of three hours waiting until the judge dismissed his case. Witness never showed up." He scratched his beard and nodded toward the coffee. "You got a good memory, Margaret. Not many people take it light and sweet."

"Oscar did," she added. "Eight cups a day. Probably why he died when he did." She opened her own cup. "You awake yet? We gotta talk."

Schaeffer leaned back on the bench and stretched his legs. "Yeah, I'm awake. What's your problem?"

"One of them is Morley," Margaret said.

"Don't let him bother you. He's been pushing a lot of numbers around these days. He's getting tired of being a lieutenant." Schaeffer sighed and took another drink. "Anything else?"

"Yes, there is something else," Margaret said. "I want you to find out about someone for me. Jason Farrell. I think he's behind some nasty business that's threatening a friend of mine." Margaret told him about the incident with the hubcap. "I want to know everything about him. You have access to information that I don't—it would take me weeks."

Schaeffer finished his coffee. "Then what?" he asked. "Write a letter to the *Times*? Guys like that don't respond to powder-puff threats."

Margaret reddened and secured her hat against the morning breeze. "Leave that to me. All I need is the information. It's a simple request."

"Yeah, like all your others. I'll see if I can fit it in. Got an address?"

Margaret gave him the information.

"If Morley finds out, he won't like it, but I'll get what I can. Then you tell me what you're planning. Just because the boss is preoccupied doesn't mean you've got a green light to get in trouble."

"Why, David," Margaret said. "Don't you trust me?" The face under the hat assumed its sweetest expression.

"About as far as I can throw one of your cookies." He winked and headed away in the direction of the youths.

Eleven

THE GRACEFUL TREES OF CENTRAL PARK reminded Angelo of the beauty of Sicily. For a moment, he was tempted to drop the heavy steel ball in his hand, lie down on the grass, and gaze up at their dancing leaves. But the little boccino was sixty feet away, and his opponent, Tagolini, was eagerly awaiting his move.

Damn that Tagolini, Angelo thought. He always throws a ball a mile. The bastard knows I have no aim past fifty feet. He swung his arm back and took a step forward. Then, in

one fluid motion, he arced his hand down and forward and
grunted as the ball sailed outward. It hit the dirt twenty-five
feet away and rolled to a stop two feet in front of the little
black ball. Angelo shook his head.

"You got to get more sleep," his good-natured opponent
laughed. "You've lost four dollars so far. This 'mano' will
make it five."

"Just throw the boccia," Angelo said. "I've still got one
more."

"Ah, but my friend, you forget it's eleven to six. All I
need is another point." Tagolini stepped into position and
studied his shot carefully while Angelo looked around him
impatiently at the open field. It was only one of many spots
in Central Park where Angelo and his cronies chose to play
their freestyle boccie. The regulation courts on Sixty-ninth
Street were usually crowded and this *campo* was much closer
to home. He heard Tagolini sweep forward and turned just
in time to see the small man release the ball. It hit a little in
front of Angelo's ball and caromed into it. When both balls
stopped rolling, Angelo's was four feet off to the side and
Tagolini's was six inches from the little black boccino.

"Boccata!" Tagolini said, making a mock bow to Angelo.
Then, trying to make his smile less expansive, he said, "Your
turn."

Angelo stepped back and picked up his second ball. It felt
heavy in his hand, heavier when he saw the target forty feet
away. He brought the ball up to eye level and dropped about
six inches into a semi-crouch. Concentrate, he told himself
as he squinted and focused on Tagolini's ball ahead of him.
He was so engrossed that he failed to see a man wearing a
thin raincoat, thin enough to reveal shoulders approximately
the size of car bumpers and a waist as thick as a middle
linebacker, approaching from the left side. The man's face
was impassive, and it was only his undeviating approach that
made Tagolini look over at him. He's probably come to watch
the game, Tagolini thought, maybe even to play. He didn't
see the knife until it was too late. The man grabbed Angelo

by the elbow and turned him around. Then he motioned to Tagolini.

"Take a walk. Turn around and he's dead."

Tagolini hesitated for a second, exchanged one terrified look with his friend, then turned and started walking. Angelo watched him until he rounded a path and disappeared behind a group of trees. The big man let his elbow go, put the knife back, and gently lifted the ball from Angelo's grasp.

"What do you want?" Angelo managed to ask. "I got eighteen, maybe twenty dollars." He reached for his back pocket.

"Keep it," the man said. "I'm here to give you something, old man, not to take it." The corners of his mouth seemed to sneer. Angelo noticed lines on the sides of his head where his wire-frame glasses bit into his skin. The man shifted Angelo's steel boccia ball idly from one hand to the other with as much effort as if he were juggling a cupcake. His face never changed expression, but the dull emptiness in his eyes said enough. Angelo didn't move.

"Yeah, Pops. Don't worry." He reached into his coat pocket and pulled out an envelope. "You got a friend who's giving you a free bus ticket to Baltimore—one way." He smiled with his mouth, but his eyes were as cold as the gleam from his glasses. "Lots of nice things in Baltimore for an old guy like you. Libraries, movies," he nodded around him, "parks. Of course, you don't have to go all the way to Baltimore—you can stop in Philly. Someone told me they got a nice zoo there." He unbuttoned Angelo's jacket and slid the envelope into his breast pocket. Then he straightened the lapels evenly.

"Your friend wants you gone," he said slowly. "Not next year, not next month." He rolled the ball back to his right hand. "Two weeks. Fourteen days. If you're not gone by then, you can kiss the world goodbye. That's not asking too much. Just a little cooperation."

"Mantex!" Angelo breathed.

"Man who? Never heard of the party." The big man looked around him and saw that they were still alone. "And

just so there won't be any misunderstanding,'' he added,
''here's a little sample—'' With absolutely no effort, he raised
the steel ball up to eye level and flicked it downward. It was
so unexpected that Angelo didn't even think to move. He
heard before he felt its impact on his left foot. There was a
small cracking noise like a chicken bone breaking, and only
then the rush of white light. Gasping, he bent over instinc-
tively while a blinding pain seared his foot and charged up
his shin. He sank to his other knee and reached out for the
ground. The white light gave way to various shades of yellow
and ochre before he could catch his breath again. By then
the man was fifty yards away and walking leisurely onto a
pathway which led out of the park. Angelo screamed out but
no one heard. He sat down and looked at his damaged foot.
Already he was feeling the pressure of the swelling. There
was no blood, no indication at all from the outside of what
damage had been done. He loosened the laces of the shoe
and tried standing. Once again the pyrotechnics flashed in
front of him and he had to sit back down. His instep throbbed,
and he thought he was going to be sick. He lay back on the
grass and closed his eyes.

''Bastards,'' he yelled, but the effort made him wince. He
looked straight up at the sky and let the nausea pass. A minute or two went by. Footsteps crunched the grass near his
head and he slowly rolled his eyes. Tagolini was bending
down, a look of concern on his face.

''What happened?'' he asked. ''He hurt you?''

Angelo sat up, then slowly, with Tagolini's help, managed
to stand.

''No, it's just my way of getting out of a losing game,''
he said with a wry smile.

''Very funny,'' Tagolini shot back. ''I called the cops.''

''I don't need the cops. I need a taxi.''

''Where you going?''

''Emergency Room,'' Angelo said. ''Unless you got a
better idea.''

Twelve

MARGARET SURVEYED THE DAMAGE THE next morning and winced. Angelo sat on the bench next to her, his foot in a white cast up to his ankle and a pair of crutches propped against his side. A worried Thelma looked on from the end of the bench.

"Guess I'm lucky," Angelo said. "I always thought they went for the kneecaps."

"How can you joke at a time like this?" Thelma asked. "They break your foot, threaten to kill you, and you sit there as though it's some little game."

"What else am I going to do?" He pulled out the ticket to Baltimore and looked at it for a minute. Then he ripped it in two and threw it over his shoulder. "Run? The last time I let someone push me around was in eighth grade. I waited until I grew a little and broke his nose in ninth grade."

"At least you could cash the ticket in." Thelma said wistfully, as she watched the two pieces of paper blow into the street.

"Not from them. I take nothing from them."

Margaret reached out and touched his shoulder.

"Here's David." She nodded toward Sergeant Schaeffer, who was about to cross the street to their little island.

"Lot of good he will do," Thelma said under her breath. "Thought you told me they weren't interested."

"Morley's not, but David's trying to help. He said he's got

some information on Farrell. Maybe when he sees what they've done—''

The light changed and Schaeffer made it across. After being introduced to Thelma and Angelo, David eased himself onto the bench next to Margaret. Before he could say anything she pointed to Angelo's cast.

''Farrell's work.''

Schaeffer raised an eyebrow.

''Smashed,'' she continued. ''One of his goons trying to convince Angelo to take a trip—bit more than harassment, wouldn't you say?''

Schaeffer frowned and shook his head. ''Sorry, Margaret, have him file a complaint.''

Angelo lit a cigarette. ''No, I'm not going to file a complaint. What good would it do? I filed a complaint when I was mugged, and all it got me was two hours of flipping through mug shots.''

''Were these the same guys?'' Schaeffer asked.

''Guy,'' Angelo corrected. ''I don't think so.''

''Well, there's not much we can do.'' Schaeffer took a small notebook from his pocket. ''You want to hear this?''

''Go ahead,'' Margaret said. ''Who is this guy Farrell anyway?''

Schaeffer opened the notebook. ''Jason Farrell, hometown boy made good. Grew up in Manhattan in the Inwood section, where he drew a couple of early arrests in the fifties. Nothing serious—hubcaps and stuff—nothing half his friends weren't doing. Graduated high school in 1955, then joined the army. Slipped in between the wars. Re-upped in '59 then was smart enough to call it quits before meeting Ho Chi Minh's buddies. In the army he seems to have distinguished himself after hours in the barracks poker games.'' Schaeffer glanced down the bench at his audience. ''This goes back a few years, mind you, but I got hold of the company roster and made a few calls. When Farrell left, he had a big enough stake to start a little investment business.''

''Investing in real estate?'' Thelma asked.

''Not yet. He started with people—'' Schaeffer looked

again at the three friends. "Jockeys to be precise. Nothing could ever be proved, but his name came up in a few investigations down South. Again, he sidestepped them just in time and left town for a while. He probably took over a quarter of a million dollars with him." Schaeffer flipped a page and waited until the noise of a passing bus subsided. "Let's see, we jump to 1970 when he comes back and sets up shop as Farrell Associates, building contractors. I don't need to tell you that to break into New York contracting you need some grease. Farrell seems to have been liberal with his Christmas and Easter presents because by 1973 he's got four projects going and is employing over sixty men. There was never any question about the jobs he did, no problems, nothing. Not until 1974, that is, and the Symons Corporation headquarters. Symons had had a $1 million-dollar interior renovation job, and Farrell Associates was the subcontractor on the walls and the ceiling work. After the job was completed, some secretary goes to hang a mirror, it happens to be the secretary who typed up all the specs, and she notices that the sheetrock is three-eighths of an inch—not three-quarters. Funny, huh? A lawsuit results, and Farrell Associates claim that they're only the subcontractors and therefore not responsible. They show work prints calling for three-eighths inch sheetrock. The general contractor denies ever sending them out and counterclaims they'd been forged. To get to the point, Farrell Associates gets a clean bill of health, and the general contractor gets hit with one hundred thousand dollars in damages." Schaeffer looked up.

"What do you think?" Margaret said.

"Don't be naive," he said, winking at her. "There's more." Schaeffer found his place in his notes and continued. "Farrell escaped damages but word got around. His business started falling off, so he figured he'd move up a notch. Those were the years—1975, 1976—when smart money was just getting into co-op and condo conversions. By then Farrell had enough to buy a few brownstones on the West Side—rundown things which he fixed up and flipped. A hundred thousand here, two hundred there. The guy was the American dream come true—''

''Yeah, from hubcaps to kneecaps,'' Margaret said, stamping out her cigarette.

''Metatarsal,'' Angelo corrected.

''Sorry.''

Schaeffer overlooked the interruption. ''But he never went in for anything really big. All his conversions are listed with the Attorney General, and they all appear to be four-story brownstones where his initial investment was small. The only problem the AG had with him was an occasional rumor of harassment in vacating some of his buildings, especially the last project. They issued warnings and it stopped.''

''We can see that,'' Thelma said in a dry tone.

''No wonder he's being so secretive about our building,'' Angelo said. ''He's on the AG's bad-boy list.''

''Then last year he stuck his neck out,'' Schaeffer continued. ''He's listed as the principal sponsor of a building called Westhaven Tower.''

''The one on Ninety-third Street?'' Margaret asked.

Schaeffer nodded. ''A twenty-story converted single-room-occupancy hotel—eighty apartments. Prices go from one hundred and seventy to a million dollars. The way I figure it, he's got an investment of from sixteen to twenty million bucks there, including all the new material he had to put in.''

''They're just starting to sell them,'' Thelma said. ''I saw they put up a big sign last week.''

''And that's Farrell?'' Margaret asked.

''Yes, and after Westhaven Tower, it looks like your building is next.'' Schaeffer closed his notebook and turned to Thelma and Angelo. ''I thought it might be interesting to check on the other properties around yours. The empty lot to the east and the garage to the west have all been optioned by a company called Santos Corporation. Sound familiar? Now, when you see that kind of stunt, it's pretty obvious what's coming.'' Schaeffer looked at the three of them. ''The next step up. Build your own. And from the size of the parcel, my guess is it's going to be something twice as big as Westhaven Tower.''

"Didn't I tell you," Thelma said, "he wants to tear down our house.''

"But can he do that?'' Margaret asked.

"Not if rent-controlled tenants are living there. That's his problem. SECTION 54, sub G of the Rent and Eviction Regulations of The City of New York.'' Schaeffer smiled. "In case you'd thought, Margaret, I was lying down on the job.''

"You, lying down on the job—?'' Margaret grinned.

"It says that if the landlord could have made a minimum of 8½-percent return on his investment he can't evict the tenants. Since it's based on the assessed valuation and not market value, almost every building in the city falls under its provision and that includes buildings with only one tenant left. It's based on the potential for rent, not the actual rent received. I think the precise language is that the landlord can't 'intentionally or willfully mismanage the property to impair his ability to earn such a return.' That means if Farrell kicked you out, you could simply protest to the district rent office, cite SECTION 54, and get your apartments back. If he wanted to appeal, it would take him months, maybe years in the courts and he'd probably lose, especially if there was a harassment complaint filed against him. The only other way would be to settle with the tenants on a straight buyout contract. I'm surprised he hasn't tried that.''

"He has,'' Margaret said. "But five thousand dollars was all he offered. I guess he figured hiring a mugger for a night was cheaper. And you're going to let him get away with it?''

"We don't know for a fact Farrell is part of Mantex or Santos. We just have your word, Margaret. His involvement with Westhaven Tower is strictly legitimate. I can talk to Morley about offering protection after what's happened, but then what? This thing can drag on for a year. You want a cop following you every time you go to the store for a pack of cigarettes?''

"What's my choice?'' Angelo asked simply.

There was a silence.

"You could move."

"No!" Angelo said. He looked over at Thelma. She shook her head, her face resolute beneath the puffy red hair.

"I'm not moving either."

"Well then—" Schaeffer said, standing up. "It's going to be a tough couple of months. I'll see what I can do." He nodded and started walking away.

"David," Margaret called.

The policeman stopped and turned around.

"Thank you."

He looked down at the three people on the bench in front of him and smiled.

"I don't know what good the information is. There's not much you can do."

"Humph, we'll see about that!" Margaret said after he left.

Thirteen

OF ALL THE FRIENDS MARGARET MET ON the Broadway benches, she saw Bertie the most often. That's because Bertie felt she had a daily responsibility to New York's pigeons. She had her favorites, but all the birds that came to the Eighty-second Street island in the afternoon were treated equally to handfuls of bread crumbs and long monologues on the state of their health. Whenever Bertie was in attendance, a moving carpet of pigeons appeared before her. That afternoon, after seeing Angelo and Thelma back home,

Margaret picked her way through the feathers and plumped herself down next to Bertie.

"Little Piccolo's been in a fight again," Bertie said, shaking her head. "I don't understand it. You'd think she'd know better by now." She pointed to a small, spotted, white-and-gray bird, and Margaret saw the ruffled scars on its neck. "It's not that she's got an aggressive personality. It's the other birds that take advantage of her." Bertie bent over and opened a hand full of crumbs in front of the little, scarred bird. She ate hungrily from the woman's palm. Then Bertie emptied the rest of the crumbs from the paper bag and watched as the flock squabbled over them.

"How you feeling today?" she asked Margaret when the action in front of them had subsided. "Seen you a lot better."

"I've got a problem," Margaret said. She brushed a pigeon off the bench between them and looked up into her friend's face. "What are you doing this afternoon?"

"Me?" Bertie smiled. "I was thinking maybe of having a late lunch at the 21 Club. What'd you think—I was going to waste my time parked on this bench all afternoon?"

"That's exactly what I thought," Margaret said, "because that's exactly what you always do." She looked at her watch. "For another hour and a half to be precise."

Bertie shifted uneasily in her loose-fitting clothes. They were usually a size too large for her ninety-eight-pound body and hung unevenly from her narrow shoulders.

"I want you to be my sister," Margaret said, straightening up Bertie's collar. "Just for the afternoon."

"Your sister!" Bertie laughed. "What on earth for?" Bertie folded the paper bag neatly and put it back in her pocketbook. Margaret had always wondered if she used the same paper bag for the crumbs, day after day, but she was too polite to ask. "Besides, you don't have a sister," Bertie said indignantly. "How am I going to pretend I'm someone that doesn't exist?"

"I know that, and you know that," Margaret said. "But they don't."

Bertie snapped her handbag closed as defiantly as she could. "Who's they?"

"The people at Westhaven Tower Apartments." Margaret smiled. "We're going to see about buying a condominium."

"You are crazy," Bertie raised her voice. "I've got enough problems getting the rent in on my place."

"No, not for real. I need some information. I'll tell you about it on the way." She stood up. "Come on, we've got to go home and get dressed up a little nicer. I'll meet you at your place in half an hour."

After one last look at her pigeons, Bertie rose from the bench. "Just this once," she said, getting up and taking hold of her friend's arm. "What's my name?"

"Let's call you Bertha," Margaret said. "But let me do all the talking."

"As always," Bertie said, and the two women turned and started crosstown.

Westhaven Tower was situated in the middle of the block between Broadway and West End Avenue in an area that was struggling to achieve a luxury residential image. The encroachment of the fast-food restaurants and late-night delicatessens had been halted at Broadway while the awnings and doormen of West End as yet hadn't made it around the corner. A sign saying, "Sales Office, twelfth floor" was plainly displayed on the awning stanchion. The lobby still showed signs of construction but the elevator's polished brass and mahogany veneer interior gleamed. The wallpaper in the upstairs hallways was a gold-flecked, paisley print. When the two women walked in through the open "sales office" door, they found themselves facing a large architect's floor plan of the various apartments.

"Can I help you?" asked a nicely dressed woman in her forties, looking up from a nearby desk. There was a hint of Britannia in her voice.

"Why, yes, dear, you can," Margaret said. "Come on, Bertha." The two women sat down in front of the agent. "We've been looking ever so long for an apartment to buy, something small and manageable.'' Margaret smiled. ''It's just for the two of us, my sister and me.'' She leaned forward and lowered her voice. ''Since our husbands died, we've been rattling around in these two large apartments—makes no sense. We thought we'd move in together.'' She looked over lovingly at Bertie. ''Start fresh—new kitchen and equipment. Especially after Herman went,'' Margaret whispered to the agent. ''It's been very hard on her, even with all the money he left.''

''Yes, of course, I understand,'' the sales agent said. ''My name is Mrs. Hart.'' She extended a hand. ''Now, what did you have in mind? A two-bedroom unit? We have the C line, with a splendid layout.'' She took a small floor plan from her drawer and passed it across the desk. ''Here's one on the fourth floor.'' She outlined the C apartment in red crayon. ''Lovely, isn't it. Only $290,000 with a fantastic common charge around $300 a month. If you buy this month, we're offering a free year's membership in our health club.''

Margaret felt Bertie's grip on her arm.

''Yes, that sounds about right,'' Margaret said, carefully inspecting the floor plan. ''I expect that with such reasonable prices you probably have a limited selection left. We really don't want to be on a low floor. So noisy, don't you know.''

''Let me see,'' Mrs. Hart said. She consulted another sheet. There were only a few lines crossed out. ''Actually we have many of the C line left. The tenth floor is gone and so is the fourteenth, but all the rest are available.'' She looked up, beaming. ''Would you like to see a model apartment?''

''Yes, of course. But before we go, I'd like to ask about the one-bedroom units. Fred, my son that is, wants to live in the same building.''

Margaret could almost see Mrs. Hart's pulse rate increase.

''The D line,'' she said. ''Wonderful space for the money. The living room is so large that many people have turned the dining alcove into a library. Here—'' and she got out a blue crayon.

''Oh, but we'd have to live on the same floor. Fred's such a help to me. If they're all taken—''

"No," the agent said quickly. "We have a few left." Again she looked at her sales sheet. "In fact, floors ten through fifteen are available. You did say you wanted to be on a high floor?"

"So many?" Margaret frowned.

"It's only because we just started selling," the agent said quickly.

"How lucky we are." Margaret leaned back and beamed at "Bertha," who was already longing to substitute her stiff handbag for the familiar crumb-filled paper one. "Tell me, Mrs. Hart, what's the neighborhood like?"

"The neighborhood—?" The agent looked as surprised as if Margaret had just asked whether the Waldorf had room service.

"This is, without doubt, the most up-and-coming neighborhood in New York. The blocks around here are all very safe, especially for older people. The food markets are just up the street and Zabar's, you've heard of them, is practically around the corner. As far as investments go, I can't think of a better area for appreciation. The neighborhood is full of doctors and writers—professional people. We don't have the kind of element you find farther north, if you know what I mean."

"No riffraff?" Margaret asked.

"Absolutely not." Mrs. Hart smiled encouragingly.

Margaret tapped Bertie on the arm. "Come, shall we see the apartment?" She stood up.

"Could I have your names first?" Mrs. Hart asked. "It's just for the logbook. And your addresses."

"Of course, I'm Freida Zeller and my sister is Bertha—" She hesitated for a second. "Bertha Piccolo." Bertie beamed. Margaret gave a West Seventy-eighth Street address.

The agent jotted down the information and then rose to her feet. "Now, I'm sure you'll just love the C line. The model is done in a more traditional decor."

"For myself," Margaret said, "I prefer modern. All that

wood gets a bit musty.'' She thought mischievously of her Victorian sofa and china figurines.

"In that case, I have a treat for you, Apartment 16A is absolutely fabulous. It's our premier duplex three-bedroom penthouse, and it's been done by the famous decorator, Sarantino. Just to show you, of course, how the modern looks in one of our spaces.'' She leaned closer. "The price tag is closer to $1 million, but the views are beautiful, especially at night.''

"I can't wait," Margaret said, grabbing onto Bertie's arm. "Come on, Bertha, let's see what a million will buy.'' Dropping back several paces behind Mrs. Hart, Margaret whispered to Bertie, "I'll make all this up to you, dear, there's a Hitchcock double feature on next week.''

Fourteen

A DAY AFTER THE INTERVIEW WITH MRS. Hart, Margaret pushed the apartment doorbell at 238 Central Park West—Jason Farrell's building. She hadn't had any problem with the doorman downstairs. One little old lady, especially one wearing a furry hat, never appeared threatening although he had called up to announce her. She was about to ring the bell again when the door opened and a large man in a dark-green corduroy suit stepped forward. He peered at Margaret through eyeglasses that were too narrow for his face.

"Mr. Farrell," she began. "I'd like to talk to you.''

"I'm not Farrell," the man said briskly. "But what's it about? If you're soliciting—"

"No, nothing like that. I've come to talk about a real-estate problem." She smiled politely and waited while the big man made up his mind.

"Come in," he said at last. "Mr. Farrell's having his hands done. He can talk for a few minutes." He motioned her through a large reception foyer, where a secretary was busy typing away, and into the living room. It was a room large enough to hold a desk the size of a Ping-Pong table and still look spacious. At the side of the desk a middle-aged woman was bending over her lotions and lacquers. Three inches away was a bowl of steaming water in which the owner of the desk was resting his right hand. Luther, the man who had admitted her, motioned to a chair and took his own seat at the side of the room. Margaret sat in the leather and chrome chair and glanced around the room. A thick white carpet covered the floor and made the modern furniture look as if it were floating. Curtains embellished with crewelwork stood on each side of the picture window that looked out onto Central Park. The walls were covered in a moiré silk fabric the color of young pears. What pictures there were had chrome frames.

"What can I do for you?" asked the man getting the manicure. "The doorman said it was something about Westhaven Tower?"

"No." Margaret looked at him steadily. He was a perfect match for his surroundings. There was an expensive gloss to his complexion and a sharp angularity to his face. His features were as dark as the smoked-glass coffee table in front of her. "No," Margaret repeated, "it's about 621 West Ninety-first Street."

"I'm afraid I don't understand," Farrell said quietly.

"I think you do, Mr. Farrell. Six hundred twenty-one West Ninety-first is the building you own through the Santos Corporation, the one you're trying to clear of tenants so you can put up a new high-rise."

Farrell took a quick glance at the other man then turned

back. "You're mistaken. The only project I'm involved in currently is Westhaven Tower. Now if you're interested in an apartment there—"

"The only thing I'm interested in," Margaret interrupted, "is in seeing that my friends are not harassed any further and thrown out on the street."

"My good woman," Farrell said pushing aside the bowl of hot water, "I don't even know your name."

Margaret hesitated. "Freunglass."

"—Freunglass." Farrell surveyed her from the top of her sweet little brown hat to the bottom of her outsized Dr. Scholl's walking shoes.

"You come barging in here with misinformation linking me to some building I've never even heard of. I don't know who you're talking about or why you chose me to accuse. Now, if you'll excuse me—"

"I will not," said Margaret stoutly. "Not until you understand that we won't take it quietly. Either you stop your harassment or you'll be sorry."

Farrell laughed. It was the kind of smug chortle that comes easily to powerful people. It momentarily deflated Margaret.

"*I'll* be sorry! Mrs. Freunglass, assuming for the minute that I am involved in whatever it is you say I am, there's no way I'd consider your threat more than the fantasy of an old lady. What could you possibly do to me—pummel me with your cane—trip me with your walker?"

Margaret reddened. "Mr. Farrell, do not underestimate us. I repeat, we will not take this abuse. I've come here to warn you." She stood up and looked down at the dark-haired man in front of her. "When you've decided you've had enough, contact me through my friends at the building." She took a step toward the door. "I don't think you realize how vulnerable you are. We've already seen through your smoke screen. That's only the beginning." She turned to go.

"I usually see my guests out," he called after her. "But not my crackpot intruders." The door slammed behind her and Farrell sat thinking for several seconds watching the manicurist lacquering his nails. Suddenly he pulled his hand away.

"Follow her, Luther. Don't let her see you." He clenched his fist. "I want to know where she lives."

"Sure thing, boss," the big man said and got up quickly.

Farrell watched him go then gave his hand back to the woman. "Damn," he said softly to himself. "How'd she find out?" The manicurist was already repairing the damage he'd done by smearing the lacquer.

Fifteen

THE FLORENCE K. BLISS SENIOR CITIZENS' center was alive with activity when Margaret arrived the next afternoon. Every Thursday was cheese-and-checkers day, and Margaret knew she'd meet most of her friends here. Admittedly, the cheese was usually some lifeless hunk of processed cheddar, but the spirited conversation that crackled across the checkerboards made up for that. When complaints about food prices failed, there was always talk of grandchildren and past trips to fill in the dead spaces between moves. She immediately saw old Pancher Reese hunched over a board studying his pieces with Solomon-like concentration. His body was so thin that the suspenders he wore appeared to be bending him in two. A wrinkled green bow tie hung limply from his collar, and his two-day-old stubble lent a whitish shadow to his cheeks. Across the table from him, Joe Durso gleefully watched as his angry opponent mumbled to himself. Durso, with his ever-present pipe sticking into the corner of his mouth and his faded tweed jacket, looked the image of the retired schoolteacher that he was. The fact that he had Pancher, the retired janitor, backed into a corner gave him great joy. He usually lost to him.

Margaret leaned toward the two men and whispered, "When you're finished, I'll be over by the coffee—something important."

Durso frowned and nodded, but he didn't remove his eyes from the board. Pancher looked up.

"What about?" he asked.

"Finish your game. I don't want to disturb you."

"If it's so important we can go right now."

"Finish the game, you weasel," Durso said.

Pancher shrugged and turned back to the board. Immediately he saw a move he hadn't noticed and shifted a piece.

"Ha," he said, looking up happily. "Take that!"

Margaret moved over to the wall where she saw her friend Rena. Rena's eyes were closed and she had an enchanted expression on her face. The cause for this, Margaret knew, was the little earplug in her ear connected to her cheap transistor. A cracker with a large smear of cheese was in her hand. Margaret nudged Rena and pointed.

"In five minutes, dear. Could you come?"

Rena looked blank. Slowly she pulled back the tangle of gray hair and plucked the earplug away.

"What's that, Margaret?"

"A meeting," Margaret said louder. "I'm getting everyone together—by the coffee in five minutes."

Rena smiled and ate her cracker. Then she repositioned her little cloth hat in the center of her tiny head. "Of course, of course." She turned back to her radio station.

That left Roosa, and Margaret knew where he would be. For a man who had a hangover every day between 10:00 A.M. and 4:00 P.M., free coffee was almost as much of a draw as a free shot of Johnny Walker Red. Margaret spotted him propped up on a little bridge chair. His eyes were only half-open and were tinted the red of cooked shrimp. A steaming cup of coffee was in his hands. Margaret sat down on the chair next to him and shook her head.

"Don't start in on me, Margaret," he said in a grumble. "I was just mourning the loss of a great man."

Margaret nodded knowledgeably. "Fiorello La Guardia again?"

" 'At's right. Best goddamn mayor this city's ever had." He took a swallow of the black liquid and made a face. "The man had heart," he said. "Fought against the Volstead Act not to mention reading the funnies to the little kids." He wiped a hand under his nose.

Margaret patted his knee. "Will you be all right in a few minutes? Sid and some of the others will be here."

"I'm always all right," he said with defiance. "Sometimes I'm just better, 'at's all." He looked down into his cup. "The coffee around here is enough to make me give up drinking."

"That'll be the day," Margaret said softly and sat back to wait.

It didn't take long. In ten minutes everyone was assembled. Durso came over with a scowl and made a point of sitting on the other side of the little circle from Pancher. Rena turned off the transistor and sat down curiously. Sid arrived and sat with Angelo and Thelma to Margaret's left. Bertie spotted the tray of crackers as soon as she walked in, unfolded her brown crumb bag, and stuffed a handful of them inside.

"Whynt'cha take some cheese, too," Roosa grumbled softly. "Choke them pigeon bastards so they won't crap over everything."

Bertie pretended she didn't hear.

The last to arrive was Rose Gaffery, Margaret's bag-lady friend. She trudged in with her eight stuffed bags, and took her time in placing them at her feet. Even though it was mid-July with the temperature hovering in the low eighties, Rose had on several sweaters and two shirts whose ragged cuffs showed. Her hair was plastered down with a solution that gave off a faint odor of cooking oil. A plain piece of twine hung around her neck on which were several keys, Rose's jewelry, worn as proudly as any Cartier choker. After settling the bags, and placing a chair for herself near Rena, Rose also made a trip to the cheese table. A minute later she came back balancing on her forearm a half-dozen canapés. After a few more moments of low murmuring, the group quieted down and turned to Margaret. Nine pairs of eyes watched as she quietly smoothed her dress and then looked up at them.

"I suppose I should begin by introducing two new friends, Angelo Varonetti and Thelma Winters." She nodded in their direction. "Two friends who are on the verge of being shamelessly kicked out into the street by their landlord. Some of you know their story. Sid and Bertie have already helped me piece it together. The events of the story have happened many times in the lives of other older people in our city without raising so much as a murmur of objection from the rest of us. This time we can't look on again while another tragedy takes place. I've asked you here together because, finally, we must do something." She looked at each one of them. "Angelo and Thelma are up against a ruthless and powerful man and our little group offers the only possible help. Alone, Angelo and Thelma are no match for their enemy and they can't continue to live the rest of their lives in fear. The answer," she said and sat back, "is to hit the man in the place where it will hurt the most—his pocketbook."

"Perhaps you should explain what's happened," Sid interrupted, "so the others will understand."

"Of course," Margaret said. "I guess I'm getting a little ahead of myself." She lit a cigarette and blew out a thin column of smoke. "Here's what we've got so far." She then recounted all the unpleasant incidents. When she was finished, there were nine angry people in front of her. "So," she said. "It has to stop and I think I know how to do it." She hesitated for a minute to take a sip of cold coffee. "We are going to turn West Ninety-third Street, a block that the sponsor of Westhaven Tower claims to be up and coming, into one that is unquestionably down and out." She smiled. "We are going to bring the flavor of the Bowery at midnight to Mr. Farrell's chic neighborhood. We are going to do it until every prospective buyer convinces himself that West Ninety-third Street is not ready for gentrification, at least not at Mr. Farrell's inflated prices. And we're going to do it by being the strangest band of characters since Fritz Lang's *M*.'' There was silence while the others looked around. Finally Durso cleared his throat.

''Are you asking us to do something illegal?''

Margaret's face was a purposeful blank. ''Not really—is it illegal to walk down a city street? Except, Roosa, you won't walk, you'll reel, preferably with one of your brown paper bags. Rose, you can spend a lot of time searching through the cans on the block. Should be enough of them to keep you busy a couple of hours per circuit.''

''Ain't nothing much good on West Ninety-third Street,'' Rose objected. ''I gave up on that block long ago.''

''Give it another try,'' Margaret said flatly. ''Bertie, you can also move your operations over there. Think the birds will come?''

''They'll go anywhere I want 'em to. Maybe not all the regulars, but in a couple of hours I should have a good flock.'' She patted her bag with the crackers inside. ''Be nice to make some new friends.''

''Just wear a big hat so the sales agent won't recognize you,'' Margaret said. She swiveled and faced Rena. ''You're always listening to opera on that radio. I think it's time for you to add your own soprano. I've heard you sing, dear, you have a lovely voice.''

Rena blushed.

''But I mean really *sing*,'' Margaret said. ''As though you were at the Met.'' Margaret beamed and turned to the others. ''See, there are things we all can do. It's not illegal to seek petition signatures on the street, either. Joe Durso, you can use the typewriter here and draw up a petition for, say, a West Ninety-third Street methadone clinic.'' She smiled. ''That will go over big with Farrell's buyers. And Sid, did you ever run a three-card monte game? Take a few hours to practice, and you'll be as good as the kids on Forty-second

Street." She lit another cigarette. "There's more, so much more—panhandling, for example. Angelo, you might even make a few bucks. See what I'm getting at? When we're finished with Mr. Farrell he'll wish he'd never heard of 621 West Ninety-first Street. He's got over $15 million tied up in Westhaven Tower, and, unless he can make sales, he's going to have to watch while that money eats him up in interest costs." She stabbed the air with her finger. "Now," she looked around again, her lively eyes taking in each one of them, "shall we give it a try?"

There was an awkward silence. Finally Thelma cleared her throat and pointed to Angelo's broken foot. "It could have been any one of you," she said. "And maybe someday it will be." She took a little embroidered handkerchief out of her sleeve and wiped a tear away. "I had so many friends there and now they're all gone." She shook her head sadly. "Please help."

"I say let's give it a shot," Sid called out. "What have we got to lose? Be a pleasure for once, giving rather than getting. I'm with you. Three-card monte, sure—and a lot more besides."

In another minute they had all agreed, even Rose.

"But how will we know if it's working?" Durso asked.

"You forget I'm a prospective client," Margaret said. "Bertie and I will call again in two weeks to see how they're doing. With all the ads they're running in the papers they should be getting a lot of lookers. We'll have to be on our toes. Let's plan on starting tomorrow morning. We can meet every afternoon on the bench on Ninety-third Street for our strategy sessions."

"Why not start now?" Roosa asked, pulling out a little pint bottle of Thunderbird wine from his inner coat pocket. "I can't wait to begin my acting career."

Sixteen

JASON FARRELL LIKED TO TAKE STEAM baths. It was one of the many whims he had satisfied when he built his office in his Central Park West apartment. In a large space that used to be a bedroom and bath, he put his Nautilus machine, his stationary exerciser bicycle, his Jacuzzi, and his steam room. It was separated from his living room-office, with its high-tech formica and chrome décor, by a simple door, but to Farrell it was another world. It was a place he could go to escape the tension of running his million-dollar real-estate business and a place that gave him almost total privacy. Almost, because he allowed a single phone inside the steam room. Now, as it rang for the third time, Farrell slowly reached for the receiver. There was a hollow, long distance sound on the line.

"Farrell, you there? It's Kravitz." The voice that came through sounded like it had been squeezed from a faulty carburetor.

"Hello, Mel, how's the weather out in Carmel?"

"Cut the gab, Farrell. What's happening to Mayberry Mews? Have I got five hundred thousand dollars tied up for nothing or what? You were supposed to have that place empty by now."

"I know, Mel, I know. I'm just running into a small problem. Nothing I can't handle." He sat back down on his marble bench, sweat pouring from his sides.

"You got another two months, Farrell, until September 21, then I pull out,'' the man from Carmel said. ''I get my five hundred grand back, and you're left holding a useless fleabag.''

''Don't worry, it'll be clear. I'm down to two apartments. You just have the other million and a half ready when I tell you. We'll need it to exercise the options on the nearby properties. The money from Westhaven Tower will be coming in soon to put me over the top. I tell you I got it all worked out.''

''That's what you told me two and a half years ago. Seems to me you're playing it pretty close to the wire. You're not getting another cent until you guarantee the building's empty.''

The steam was getting to Farrell. He thought he should play it tougher. ''If you're going to turn your back on a free fifteen percent share in a real-estate gold mine that's your goddamn business,'' he managed. ''I'll get the dough elsewhere.''

''Yeah, like you came crawling for the original five hundred thousand bucks. Without me, Farrell, you're cooked on this one and you know it. Fifteen percent of nothing is still nothing—always was and always will be.'' A nasty chuckle traveled through the wire and sent chills down Farrell's spine in the 140-degree room. ''September 21— remember? If you don't have an empty building when our mortgage expires, I take my money back. No extensions. You don't have my money, I get very angry, you understand? I still got plenty of friends in New York.''

''Listen, Mel, everything will be all right. Trust me. I got Westhaven together, didn't I?'' He waited for the other man's reply but the phone went dead. Farrell cursed and slammed his end down.

''Son-of-a-bitch!'' He had to stand under his ice-cold needle shower for three minutes before he regained his composure. Ten minutes later, he was dressed and behind his desk.

''Luther,'' he yelled at the big man sitting with his eyes closed by the picture window, ''what the hell's happening with that Varonetti guy at 621 West Ninety-first?''

Luther, took a moment to concentrate. "The old guy I hit the other day?"

"Yeah, precisely."

"Nothing, boss, you told me to give him two weeks to move. Ain't been but a coupla days."

Farrell breathed hard. "Well, make sure he's out in time, damn it! I don't care how you do it—and the old lady, too. This bullshit has got to stop." He slammed his fist down and looked out the window. "Just like a bunch of old loonies to hold up progress like this."

Seventeen

MARGARET AND BERTIE WATCHED AS Roosa and Sid shuffled off down the block. This was the second day of "Operation Condo Kill," as Durso had dubbed it, and they were just getting into the swing of things. Rose was already in place picking through the garbage cans, and Rena was doing her loudest rendition of Musetta's Waltz from *La Bohème*. They had decided to try three-hour shifts before returning to the bench on Ninety-third Street for a replacement. Margaret wanted four people on the block at all times during the day. She knew that the real buyers would stay inside for a longer time, come back often, and give the neighborhood a close inspection. She told her friends to keep an eye open for people who fit that pattern.

"You hungry, dear?" Margaret asked Bertie as she saw the hot dog cart at the corner.

Bertie shook her head. "My feet are killing me. At least

on the benches I can sit when I feed my birds. I'm going home and lie down for a couple of hours. See you later.'' She got up and trundled across the street. Margaret waited until the light changed and crossed over to the little wagon with the big yellow-and-blue umbrella. It was like every other hot dog wagon in New York except that the vendor happened to be a woman. Margaret smiled when she saw her.

"Morning, Mrs. Sanchez,'' Margaret said to the tiny woman with a pair of tongs in her hand. ''What are you doing so far uptown?''

The woman returned the smile. ''Ran out of knishes. The Eighties are better for knishes, the Nineties better for hot dogs.'' She tapped the tongs on the stainless steel in front of her. ''And you?''

Margaret looked at her watch and said idly, ''Oh, visiting. I guess it's lunchtime. You still got some knockwurst?''

The woman flipped open a lid and peered into the oily hot water inside. Then quickly she fished with the tongs and came up with a large sausage.

''The usual?'' she asked and Margaret nodded. Very carefully she slipped the knockwurst into an oversized roll and traded the tongs for a long sharp carving fork sticking out of a container of sauerkraut. She stabbed the mound of steaming sauerkraut, transferred a mass of it onto the meat, and, after wrapping the roll in a napkin, handed it over. Margaret gave her a dollar.

''Best wurst on the street,'' Margaret said. ''Too bad I can't eat it more often. It's bad for my stomach.''

Mrs. Sanchez beamed and pocketed the money. ''I wish I had more customers like you. If I see the same face twice a month, it's unusual.''

Margaret was going to add something when a man came up and asked loudly for two hot dogs with mustard and onions. Instead, she waved goodbye to Mrs. Sanchez and walked back to the bench on the island. She sat down next to Sid and waited until he turned a page of his paper.

''How's it going?''

''Not so good,'' he said without taking his eyes off the

paper. "I almost had the triple at Roosevelt last night, but I was too chicken to wheel the first two horses." He grimaced. "Three hundred eighty-five dollars!" He snapped the paper shut. "I could shoot myself."

Margaret paused while she took a bite of the wurst and savored it. "I was not referring to your horses," she said. "I was thinking about your morning's shift—you know, the three-card monte?"

"Oh that," Sid said and grinned. "Sixty dollars up. Like taking candy from a baby—let me show you."

"That's not necessary," Margaret said primly. "I'm more interested in what's going on at Westhaven."

"That's where I got the sixty," Sid said. He sat back and watched as Margaret took another bite. "I was down towards the end of the block when I spot this natty little guy coming out. He had floor plans and all the literature and a look on his face like he'd just seen Shangri-la. I'd seen him there before, so I figured he was a potential buyer. Before he was thirty feet away, I had my cardboard table on top of the garbage can, the three cards spread out, and a spotless twenty right in front. It was such an inviting setup, I could have stopped the Pope. Of course, by the time he got to me he had spotted Roosa slumped over the fender of a car and had to wade through Bertie's pigeons. Well, he sees the setup and slows down. 'Twenty will get you forty,' I said and start moving cards. 'Just find the red one.' I make it so obvious that a blind inchworm could spot it. He plays, takes my twenty, and starts walking away. 'Forty'll get you eighty,' I call out and he swings around. But this time I do an underhand drop and he's a mile off." Sid chuckled. "That hooked him. He dropped another forty before he gave up. He looked madder than a whitewashed hornet. He makes it to the end of the block where Angelo stops him with his petition. The poor guy turns around, sees the three of us, then drops all his paperwork in the nearest garbage can. There's one apartment we skunked. If we keep it up, we'll have them eating out of our hand."

"One little success does not a victory make," Margaret

said grinning. "But it sure makes me feel good. Keep it up—by all means." Margaret finished the rest of the wurst and glanced at her watch. "New shift just went on a half-hour ago. You're not on for another couple of hours." She brushed the crumbs off her skirt. "You feel like taking in a movie at the Thalia?"

Sid smiled and opened his paper. "You caught me in the middle of some important deliberations. I got to make up for yesterday's lapse."

"Seems to me," Margaret said standing up, "that with your three-card monte, you won't need to bet the horses."

"Not need to bet on the horses!" Sid was scandalized. "There is no need greater than hitting the triple. It's nothing less than a reaffirmation of the human intellect. It's good triumphing over evil." He snapped his paper open. "Women!" he said and buried his head. She turned and as delicately as she could, walked away.

Eighteen

ANGELO TRIED THE NUMBER FOR THE fourth time. Standing in the hot telephone booth with traffic racing by him, he thought for a moment that he should forget the whole business. After all, he hadn't spoken to Donghia in over a year. Then, miraculously, the line was answered and he found himself speaking to Donghia. At first he stuttered and sounded foolish. Donghia calmed him down. "What is it, my old friend?" he asked quietly in his native Sicilian dialect. "Why have you called?"

Angelo stopped stuttering, took a deep breath, and then he made his request. "I gotta come up and see you. I need— I need a little help."

Donghia laughed. "For over fifty years I've known you, Varonetti, and never one request. So now, I feel maybe you've gotta right. You've waited long enough. I don't even need to know what it is you want. You know the address—you come up, you get it."

Angelo thanked him and said he'd be there in an hour. He looked at his watch. That would give him plenty of time to get back for the final shift. All this with Westhaven Tower was fine, he thought, but there came a time when you had to take stronger measures, and the end of the two weeks was drawing closer. Donghia, he would know what to get him. He lit a cigarette, opened the phone booth, and hobbled out in the direction of the subway.

Donghia's address on Carmine Street hadn't changed in thirty years. He lived on the top floor over his bakery in an apartment that always had the slightly intoxicating aroma of freshly baked bread. It was an apartment he claimed he wouldn't trade for the best one on Park Avenue. It had seen the growing up of his two daughters and thirty years of affectionate quarreling with their mother. It had also been the nerve center of a little local business that dealt not in flour and shortening but in controlled substances. Donghia owed his success in the bakery to his liberal use of butter, and in his drug business to a resolute lack of ambition. For thirty years, he had been content to stay in a small area north of Canal Street and west of Sixth Avenue. He was uninterested in anything outside this location. On his own turf, he knew who was overdrawn on his Master Charge account, who was due for a raise, and, more important, who had a continuing and necessary interest in his special commodity.

His was a retail operation and he was happy to keep it that way. He made enough money to get a new car every year and keep his daughters' Bergdorf Goodman accounts up to date. He also had a little left over for friends who he would gladly help. In fact, when Angelo was shown into the living room, that's what he thought he had come for. After all, since their early days together on New York's Federatione Siciliano soccer team, Varonetti had always been short of money but too proud to ask his rich friend for it.

"I'll get right to the point," Angelo said. "I need a gun— nothing fancy—just something simple that shoots."

Donghia leaned back and stared at his old friend.

"No, you got to be kidding," he said finally. "You wouldn't even know how to use it."

"I can learn," Varonetti said.

"But what you gonna do with it, shoot pigeons?"

Angelo reddened then stood up. "So, I'm sorry I came. Maybe it was a stupid idea."

"Sit, sit," Donghia motioned. "Why should I question what's on your mind. If you want to commit suicide there are cleaner ways. If you want to murder someone you're old enough to have good reasons." Donghia sighed heavily and reached for a drawer to his right. He fumbled around inside until he came up with the gun, a dark, snub-nosed revolver. He placed it on the desk in front of Varonetti.

"I wouldn't do this for everyone," he said. "But a promise is a promise. This one here, it's kind of a utility piece, but in case you do something uh—improper with it," Donghia smiled, "do me a favor and throw it in the river. Best way is the ferry." He stood up and came around to place a hand on Varonetti's shoulder. "I wouldn't want the police asking too many questions. You understand?"

Angelo nodded.

"Now, if you need more help, I mean besides the piece—"

Varonetti shook his head. "This is my problem." He reached out tentatively for the gun and lifted it. He heard a click, and Donghia flinched as the muzzle of the revolver swung past his stomach. He reached out and steadied Angelo's hand.

"You just took off the safety catch. Be careful. These things ain't so accurate." He moved back to his desk.

Angelo stood up and put the gun in his jacket pocket. "I'll bring it back."

"Just don't shoot yourself in the other foot."

Angelo headed toward the door. "You always did have good advice. Sometimes I wonder why I never worked for you."

"You couldn't bake and you wouldn't break heads, that's why."

"Yeah," Angelo said. "Well, I still can't bake. Thanks." He turned and pushed the door open. Donghia heard him hobbling down the stairs all the way to the first floor.

Nineteen

ROBERT (BINKY) MCPHERSON AND HIS wife, Cindy, were arguing on their way down in the wood-veneered elevator. It was a polite argument, not one given to raised voices or wild gestures. In fact, the last wild gesture Binky had made was two years earlier when he found out that his son, Robert Jr., had been arrested on a drunk and disorderly charge. But the issue today was not one of family embarrassment, it was simply whether to put down a deposit on the sweet little two-bedroom apartment Cindy had found. Ever since Robert Jr. had gone off to Colgate a year earlier, Cindy had been trying to persuade her husband to purchase an apartment and at last she had succeeded. The big house in Westchester seemed lifeless without their son, and there were enough problems in a small advertising agency without having to deal with Amtrak every day.

Cindy had little doubt that her husband would eventually come through with the thirty-thousand-dollar deposit to secure apartment 8F in Westhaven Tower. Compared with everything else she had seen, Westhaven Tower was ideal. There was even an oblique view of the Hudson which would make her friends at the Tuesday bridge game quite envious. It was brand-new and convenient to her mother who lived only eight blocks away. The only possible problem was the mixed neighborhood, but they were assured it was going to be the block of the future. Her trump card, and the feature that she knew would convince her husband, was the health club on the roof. Binky hadn't stopped beaming since he had glimpsed the sauna and hot-tub installation twenty minutes earlier.

"Then why not give them the money now?" Cindy asked in exasperation as the elevator door opened. "If we wait too long someone will take our apartment."

"I didn't notice any lines," Binky said, pointedly brushing a piece of lint off his checked trousers. "But you're right, Cici, I like it. It's just a lot of money, that's all. I think we should walk around, have a cup of coffee—"

"We have only ten minutes on the meter."

"You want me to spend three hundred thousand dollars, but you can't put another dime in a goddamn parking meter?"

Cindy fell silent. She knew Binky well enough to know when he'd been hooked. So, give him a half-hour, she thought. They walked arm in arm to the front door. "Maybe a red rug in the living room," she said as they reached the pavement.

"Maybe. Be a good match for the curtains."

Cindy grinned as they turned toward Broadway. "Not even half an hour—fifteen minutes," she said softly to herself.

"What's that smell?" Binky asked all of a sudden. His wife stopped and looked around. Ten feet ahead of them, she spotted an old woman unwrapping a foul-looking scrap of paper. From the inside of it she pulled a piece of fish that could not have been alive two weeks earlier. At the moment,

the rancorous fumes would have emptied Radio City Music
Hall in three minutes. As they watched, Thelma held the
half-eaten fish out at arm's length and started walking toward them.

"Here, kitty, kitty," she mewed and bent low to look
under the parked cars. "Here, kitty."

Binky and his wife were so stunned that they stood still.
The closer Thelma came, the more difficult it was for them
to break the spell. Thelma stopped two feet away.

"You folks seen little Gulliver? She's here every day about
this time." Thelma stared up at them with a roundness to
her eyes that invited pity. The stench surrounding her was so
thick as to be almost visible.

"Little scrawny red thing. Weren't for me, she'd go hungry."

Finally Binky acted. Without saying anything, he tugged
his wife around and walked away. For the next thirty yards
Cindy alternately walked and coughed into her handkerchief.
When they looked back the old woman was still searching
under the cars, but the fish was now in the middle of the
pavement.

"God, what was that?" Binky said. His wife didn't have
a chance to answer. From seemingly out of nowhere an old
man glided up with red suspenders and a sign on his chest.
"Save our Nation's Buffalo," it read. A placard on his gritty
felt hat echoed the sentiment. "Buffaloes Made This Country Great."

"Can I interest you people in a free pamphlet describing
the plunder and destruction of one of our most important
natural resources?" the old man asked.

Cindy edged away nervously.

"Now, lady, I know you think this isn't as important as
the Dolphin Movement," Pancher said fervently. "But whoever heard of Davy Crockett eating dolphin steaks?"

There was nowhere to go but across the street. Binky followed his wife and almost got clipped by a cruising gypsy
cab.

"I don't believe it," Binky said and looked back at the

man who was harmlessly walking up the street. Cindy didn't know whether to cry or laugh. The decision was made for her by Durso who sidled up to them as they stood looking at Pancher's receding figure.

"Digitals," he whispered. "I got digitals."

Binky was almost afraid to look. But when he turned around he saw a perfectly normal-looking older gentleman in a tweed jacket. Perfectly normal, that is, until he looked closer and saw that one of the sleeves on his jacket was pushed up to his elbow revealing a pasty-looking forearm with fifteen watches on it. If Binky had looked closer, he would have seen that, in fact, only one was a digital and the others were so old they'd long since ticked their last second. It made no difference; the sight was so startling that Binky inadvertently pointed to the arm.

"Yes, I can let you have that one," Durso whispered. "Genuine Rolex. Gimme fifty bucks." He looked around and lowered the sleeve suspiciously. "You want it—? Okay." Durso raised the sleeve again quickly. "Take another look, but forty's the lowest I'll go."

Cindy took a quick look at her husband and saw in that instant that it was not to be. All that she had worked for, that fragile web of suggestion, envy, and fantasy that she'd hoped would culminate in apartment 8F at Westhaven Tower, was as dead in the water as an oil-slicked pelican. She burst into tears at the same moment Binky grabbed her arm to lead her away. "By my watch we still have three minutes," he said angrily, "before we lose our dime!"

Twenty

TWO WEEKS AFTER THEIR FIRST VISIT, Margaret and her "sister" Bertha went back to visit Mrs. Hart. This time Bertie was wearing her nicest dress and matching feather hat. Any resemblance to the woman who had been feeding pigeons in front of Westhaven Tower would have been considered purely coincidental.

"Come on, Bertha," Margaret urged as they marched over to the sales desk. The office was empty except for Mrs. Hart and a little kitten curled up on a windowsill.

"Hello again," Mrs. Hart beamed. She quickly riffled through her small index file. "Mrs. Zeller and Mrs. Piccolo, isn't it? Have you made a decision?"

"What we were really wondering about is pets," Margaret said after settling herself in her chair. "You see, several buildings we've visited won't allow them and, well, Bertha here is especially fond of little animals."

"But of course. There's no difficulty about pets. As long as they're not man-eaters." Mrs. Hart coaxed out a flat laugh. "You see, we've already got a mascot." She pointed to the little kitten. "In fact—we encourage it." She opened a drawer and withdrew a deposit form. "No problem at all."

"And then," Margaret leaned forward and gave the younger woman her most compelling smile, "we're getting on in years, you know, and were wondering about, well—safety." Margaret looked over at Bertie. "Isn't that right, dear?"

Bertie nodded. "I told my sister—living in such an empty building—"

"Makes one hesitate," Margaret completed the thought. "See what we mean? Two old ladies all alone. Empty corridors." She sat back and fixed Mrs. Hart with a questioning look. "But I told Bertha that by now more apartments have been sold—enough to make us feel secure."

"But surely your son on the same floor—"

"No," Margaret said. "He works all day."

"And the television surveillance in the elevators?" the agent prompted.

"Don't trust electronic gizmos," Bertie said. "People make the building safe. Haven't been mugged in forty years where I live because there's always someone in the elevator going somewhere."

"All it would take would be another couple of people on the floor and maybe a few more sprinkled downstairs—certainly not the whole building," said Margaret.

After a pause, Mrs. Hart said reluctantly, "Well, let's see." She pulled out the master sheet and opened it flat on the table. Margaret leaned forward. There were still the same number of apartment listings crossed off in red pencil, perhaps ten in all.

"You do realize we've only been open a few weeks," Mrs. Hart said as she studied the figures. "When the ads take hold there will be a lot of traffic. If anything, I'd say you're here at the best time."

"Still the same number as last time," Bertie muttered, sitting back.

"Nothing else sold?" Margaret asked innocently.

"Oh, there will be sales. There's a nice couple from Westchester who are about to put down a deposit as well as several prospective buyers. Believe me, now is the best time."

Margaret pulled her handbag closer. "I don't know."

Mrs. Hart leaned across her desk and lowered her voice. "And if you act now, I *think* we might be able to make it easier, but don't quote me."

"Make what easier?" Margaret asked, frowning.

"Maybe the financing, or if you don't need financing, maybe the price. Let's see. You were interested in the C line—eleventh floor." She studied another piece of paper. "It's listed at three hundred thousand dollars. Now we can't change the common charge, but maybe I could convince the sponsor to drop it a little, say to $285,000." She looked up speculatively at the two older women sitting across the desk from her. Margaret's eyes flickered, but that was the only sign she got. "But you'd have to act now. A deposit of $28,5000 would hold the apartment until the papers could be drawn up. I'm sure we could work out the same discount for your son's apartment."

Margaret looked over at Bertie. "What do you say, dear? It's a savings of $15,000."

Bertie, without hesitation, shook her head, no. "Too soon," she said. "I don't want to live in a morgue—probably wind up in one."

Margaret looked back at Mrs. Hart and shrugged. "I guess we'll wait. We'll come again next week. Maybe by then—" She stood up and helped Bertie to her feet. "You do understand. You have to worry about the little things when you get on in years."

Mrs. Hart sighed and walked them to the elevator. "You're sure that you want to wait?" she asked as the door opened.

"Yes, for now," Margaret answered. They turned and stepped inside. As the elevator moved downstairs, Margaret squeezed her friend's hand. "You were very good, dear," she said. "Especially that line about the morgue."

Bertie adjusted her little feather hat. "Of course. I practiced it just like you said."

Twenty-one

FOR THE NEXT SEVERAL DAYS THE LITTLE group of friends kept up their offensive. Roosa found he had particular success posing as a panhandler, especially when he doggedly followed people down the block. On two occasions he heard people say that perhaps West Ninety-third Street was not the best neighborhood to buy into.

When things were active upstairs in the sales office, the little group came as close as they dared to the front door. A few times, people just spotted them and didn't even bother going inside. Rena was struggling for her high notes with abandon and had even choreographed a few modest dance steps to go with the singing. Rose, exceeding even her wildest ambitions, was now waddling around with no less than ten shopping bags. Most of the time she was a veritable roadblock. Standing in the center of her possessions in her three layers of sweaters, an old woolen cap, a faded skirt, and unlaced, high-topped basketball sneakers, she would shunt foot traffic around her with masterful indifference. Sid abandoned the three-card monte the first week in favor of his first love. Whenever he was on the block, he surrounded himself with two or three friends from the OTB office and spent his shift talking, touting, and handicapping the races. He did this in a voice loud enough to attract the attention and disparaging stares of the non-bettors emerging from Westhaven Tower.

All in all, the ''condo killers'' appeared to be greatly successful. After another week, Margaret revisited Mrs. Hart and learned that there had been no further sales. This took place after *The New York Times* ran a half-page advertisement for Westhaven Tower calling it "the luxurious alternative." Margaret, far from being over-confident, planned to wait another week before making her follow-up call on Farrell.

"A month with no sales would be devastating to him," Margaret said to Sid that night at their meeting bench, "and a powerful bargaining point for us. After all, he sold close to a dozen apartments in the two weeks before we began. Nothing could be more clear—he'll have to listen to our demands. There're too many of us."

"I hope you're right," Sid said and went back to figuring the odds on a B/E Daily Double selection at Aqueduct.

Twenty-two

MRS. HART WAS VERY DISCOURAGED. THE commission arrangement she had worked out with Farrell was way below the normal brokerage fee, and she had accepted it on the safe assumption that the volume of sales would compensate her. But the volume of sales in the last few weeks wouldn't even pay for her box of crayons. She was expected to open the office at 8:30 A.M. every day and close it at 5:30 P.M. She had to send out for lunch or bring it with her, lest she miss one precious customer. It was not surprising then, that cooped up in her office, she had no idea of what was happening in the street. She did, however, realize that something was wrong. After ten years in the New York real-estate market, she had a strong sense of when clients were all set to buy and when they were just looking. She had been convinced six times in the last two weeks that she'd have binder money before the day was out, and six times she'd been disappointed. Once, she could understand, maybe twice. She got up, walked to the window, and looked out in dismay. From where she stood she could barely see the pavement in front of the building way below her. Her office was empty and there was no one entering the building. She didn't have to look at her watch to know she was hungry.

"The heck with it," she muttered. "One decent hot lunch—half an hour at most." She took the phone off the hook, quickly locked the door and took the elevator downstairs. She was thinking of a juicy cheeseburger as she spun out into the street. But she never made it farther than five yards up the block. She was shocked by the enormous group of pigeons she saw fluttering around the old woman by the curb.

They shouldn't allow this, she thought. No wonder it's so hard to sell apartments. Then she looked intently at the woman distributing the bread crumbs. She was about to go over and say something indignant when her mouth opened in surprise.

It can't be, she thought, taking a step closer. At that instant Bertie looked up and stared in the woman's direction. A look of fright came over her and she quickly turned away—but not quickly enough. Mrs. Hart stifled a little cry and retreated back to the entrance of the building. On the way, she spotted in one panoramic sequence Rose, Roosa, and Durso. It took her only two minutes to make it back upstairs to her phone.

"I think we have a problem here," she said in a breathless voice when Farrell answered.

"Of course we have a problem," he said angrily. "No sales in three weeks. I'd say we have more than a problem."

"No, but—" Mrs. Hart hesitated. "I think I've found the reason for it. I think there's something deliberate going on."

"Deliberate? What do you mean?"

"Perhaps you'd better come over and see for yourself. I may be jumping to conclusions, but—" again she hesitated. "There's this crazy bunch of old people—"

There was silence on the line. "I'll be right over," Farrell said quietly. Mrs. Hart sat back to wait.

Roosa had never seen Farrell before so when this well-dressed businessman started to angle in toward the front door of Westhaven Tower, he decided to go into action. He met up with him eight feet from the entrance.

"Got a quarter, buddy?" Roosa slurred. "Cuppa coffee."

Farrell looked him over with an unmistakable loathing and said, "Get the hell out of here."

"Iss a free country," Roosa said and stumbled into him. Farrell pushed him back. "Quarter's all I want, Mac. Gimme a buck and I won't bother you the rest of the week." Roosa burped and followed it with a sheepish grin. Farrell looked around for a doorman before he remembered they weren't scheduled to start until after the lobby was finished. He grabbed Roosa's collar and marched him down the block. At the corner he released him.

"Get your ass out of here," Farrell said. "Go panhandle somewhere else." He turned back to the building and stepped angrily inside.

Mrs. Hart greeted him with her conclusion. "It's those old tramps downstairs. There were four of them this afternoon. One of them keeps coming back to check on our sales progress posing as a buyer—her name is Mrs. Piccolo."

"A buyer!"

Mrs. Hart reddened. "She gets dressed up when she comes. Did you see her? She's the one with the pigeons."

"All I saw was a wino," Farrell said flatly. He was silent for a minute. "That scheming old bitch," he muttered and slammed his fist down on the desk. Mrs. Hart jumped in surprise. "Don't worry, they'll be gone by this evening." He reached for the phone and dialed quickly.

Twenty-three

BY THE TIME LUTHER ARRIVED ON THE
block an hour later, Bertie and her pigeons had been replaced
by Thelma and her fragrant fish. Pancher stood a few feet
away with his "Save Our Nation's Buffalo" sign on his chest.
Roosa was still weaving unsteadily by the cars near the awning and Rose was working on a garbage can four doors away.
Luther went for Roosa first. Without saying a word, he hit
the older man a blow just below his sternum. Roosa dropped
like a stone.

"Clear out," he said loudly over Roosa's gasping body.
"Next time you won't be so lucky." He turned and walked
the few steps to Rose. "You, too, you old witch." He kicked
one of her bags. The paper ripped and a shower of string,
Styrofoam cups, hair curlers, half-smoked cigarettes, and
other assorted street finds scattered across the pavement.
Rose looked aghast at what he had done. "Here, stop that!"

But Luther moved on to several of the other bags and up-
ended them around her feet. Old magazines tumbled out and
started blowing in the wind. He kicked at them until they
tore into ragged pieces. Then he saw a little gilt-edged mirror
and stepped on it. Rose let out a shriek and lunged for him.
Luther neatly took a step back and caught Rose by the throat.
He tightened his grip and pushed her back. "Off the block,"
he said. "You and the rest of this scum. If I see you here
again I'll get really nasty." He released her with a little shove
and turned around. He saw it coming and tried to duck, but

Thelma's rotten fish glanced off his forehead with a squishing sound.

"Run Pancher—get the police," Thelma yelled, dancing out of Luther's reach to the opposite side of a parked car. The fish clouded his eyes and he had to blink for about a minute before he could see again. Then the stench took over, and Luther, big as he was, bent over coughing and gasping. During the brief delay this caused, Pancher made it to Broadway.

Margaret was sitting on her "operations" bench at Ninety-third when she saw Pancher with his sign scurry across. There was a look of panic on his face. "We gotta get a cop. Some guy's attacked Roosa and now he's starting in on Rose and the others," he said breathlessly.

Margaret crossed the street in the direction of the building. She pointed to a telephone on the corner. "I think it's 666-4980—that's Morley's number—it'll be faster than 911. Tell him what you saw." She waited only long enough to see Pancher come up with a quarter before rushing down the block. As she approached her three friends, Roosa lay groaning on the pavement, Thelma was still shielding herself behind a parked car, and Rose was watching in utter dismay as Luther continued tearing into her bags. He held an overstuffed plastic sack over his head and repeatedly brought it crashing down onto the sidewalk. A little transistor radio came spilling out through one of the rips, smashing into several pieces as it hit the cement. A compact with chalky face powder let loose its contents, dusting the air in a long arc as he flung the bag away.

Margaret moved closer without knowing what to do. She looked behind her up the block but no policemen were coming. When she turned back, the big man was heading for Rose, his hand clenched into an ugly fist. Nobody else was on the street to stop him, so Margaret did the first thing that came to mind—she pushed him. But Luther didn't fall. He just took a single step to regain his balance. Then he turned and looked curiously at his new victim, placing her immediately as the old lady from Farrell's office. He smiled wickedly and took a step forward—right into Margaret's swinging handbag. Her timing was perfect. The corner of the heavy bag caught Luther on the mouth, and the force of the blow shattered the bottle of cologne she always carried inside. Luther staggered and put a hand up to his bloody face. Shaking his head to clear it, he then looked at Margaret. She saw his eyes narrow with concentrated rage. In one motion, he reached into his pocket and withdrew a slender knife. It flashed open as he started for her again, but Margaret was already several feet away, running as fast as her stubby old legs could carry her. She crossed the side street, just before a file of cars, and headed for Broadway. She could hear him bellowing, his footsteps sounding behind her like explosions. She wanted to turn around and look, but she knew that was wrong. Keep running, she told herself, until you feel the arm around your neck. Maybe something would happen—but it was too late. She felt a tugging on her handbag. She let go of the bag and tensed for the awful pain she knew was coming. But still her legs kept her moving. On her left, she saw the door of a store open. The flesh on her back jumped in anticipation of the knife, but instead she heard a loud thump like the sound of a stack of newspapers falling off a truck. Unable to keep from glancing behind her any longer, she saw a dazed Pancher and his "Save Our Nation's Buffalo" sign sprawled against the building line. The sign had a noticable split down the middle. Then she saw her attacker lying on the pavement at the base of a parking meter. His knife had skittered under the nearby car, but the collision had only stopped him momentarily. Even as she watched, the big man rose to one knee and steadied himself against the stanchion. His eyes fastened on hers again, and a look of raw hatred flashed out. He took a few seconds to catch his breath and began to stand up. The hand that had held the knife now clenched into the hammerlike fist. Margaret stifled a little scream and turned around.

I can't run anymore, she told herself but the message never got to her legs. She started out again, irrationally, because now she was so exhausted she could hope to go only a few yards—maybe to the end of the block. She looked. There at the edge of the crosswalk, twenty yards away, was the little wagon with the yellow-and-blue umbrella. Mrs. Sanchez was peering into her steaming vat of water and checking on her inventory. No one ever looked so good to Margaret. Ten yards, five yards, and then she was there. She grabbed onto the handle of the wagon and spun around it. Mrs. Sanchez was about to say something when she was pushed out of the way by the big man. Margaret reached into the sauerkraut container and withdrew the sharp carving fork.

"That's far enough," Margaret gasped and held the fork out in front of her. She steadied herself with her other hand on the cart. Luther hesitated and looked down at the fork still dripping with sauerkraut.

"Who are you kidding, old lady?" Luther sneered and leaned forward. Margaret stabbed the air in front of him and made him straighten.

"For fifty years I've been carving brisket of beef," she said hoarsely. "I don't think you'd be any different. This will make a nasty wound—two in fact."

The blood still trickling from both sides of Luther's mouth made him look like a carnival clown, a vengeful Emmett Kelly. His fists opened and closed in frustration as he tried to size up the best way to get at her. It wouldn't take long before a little knot of onlookers formed. Luther faked left and lunged to his right. It was a clumsy move made more so by his having to negotiate the end of the cart. Once again Margaret's fork flashed out, but this time it struck. One of the prongs sank into the skin at the base of his thumb and he yelled in pain. He drew his hand back and looked at the neat little wound. "Son-of-a-bitch!" he cursed.

It was a standoff, and the two stood glaring at each other for several seconds. Finally, Margaret spoke again. "You tell Farrell if he wants to get rough, so will we." She bravely stirred the air in front of her with the fork. "We've got an ex-barber and a retired butcher, and next time we won't be so careless. There are no laws against getting petitions signed, feeding stray cats, or looking in garbage cans. And from now on, I'm going to make sure there's a cop on the block to keep it that way. Tell Farrell if he wants to come to some compromise, to leave a message at 621 West Ninety-first Street.''

Luther glowered at her, but the gathering noise from down the block told him he should take off. Without turning to look, he raced away across Broadway.

Margaret sighed, and the arm holding the fork dropped limply to her side. It was several seconds before she could comprehend the voices around her. When she looked up she saw Pancher, Mrs. Sanchez, and Sergeant Schaeffer. They were all talking at once, but Schaeffer's voice was the loudest.

''Who was it?''

Margaret shrugged. ''I don't know his name. He works for Farrell.''

''I've called an ambulance for the others,'' Schaeffer continued. He looked at Margaret apologetically. ''I went to Ninety-third Street and Broadway first because that's where I got the call. Here, I think this is yours.'' He handed her back a handbag reeking of spilled cologne.

Margaret said ''thank you'' to Schaeffer and then turned to address Pancher. ''That was very brave of you colliding with him like that. You saved my life.''

Pancher blushed. ''I couldn't let him catch you. Besides,'' he said with a grin, ''I had a half-inch of plywood protecting me. Even so,'' he rubbed his chest, ''I feel as though I'd just had an argument with an A train.''

''Here,'' Mrs. Sanchez said cheerily. ''Have a sausage. It'll make you feel better.'' As she fished for the sausage in the oily water, she told him how she had run down the block to get help and bumped into Schaeffer outside his patrol car.

''By the time we got back, you'd already scared the man off,'' she concluded, handing the wurst over to Pancher. He took it gratefully.

''The knife,'' Margaret said suddenly. ''It's probably under that car where he fell. Maybe you could get a fingerprint.'' She pointed to the middle of the block, and Schaeffer walked over. When he came back he was holding a thin stiletto in a handkerchief.

"Nasty little item," he said. "I'll run it over to the lab." Just then the sound of a siren filled the street, and an ambulance turned down toward Westhaven Tower.

"I want to see," Margaret said. "I hope they're all right." She started to turn in the direction the ambulance had gone.

"Hold on a minute," Schaeffer said. "I've got to make a report. I'm afraid you'll have to come in."

"That's just what I was going to suggest," Margaret said. "But first there's something I've got to do."

Twenty-four

A SHORT TIME LATER, MARGARET, BERTIE, and the other members of their little clan were seated in the corner booth of Squire's Coffee Shop. Margaret, looking calm and composed again, scanned the faces of her friends, letting her gaze rest affectionately on Bertie's set features. "How are you feeling now, dear?" she asked, leaning across the table.

"I don't know about them," Bertie nodded around the table, "but I'm scared. Roosa's still having trouble breathing even though the guy in the ambulance said he'd be all right. I don't think any of us counted on it getting this serious."

"That's right," Roosa said, and by way of confirmation went into a mild paroxysm of coughing.

Margaret waited until he was through before speaking. "I understand," she said. "Running into opposition always makes one stop and think. But just the fact that Farrell sent that thug must tell you something. We're having a real effect, otherwise he wouldn't have taken notice.''

"But Margaret," Durso said, looking professorily at his pipe, "now that he has, as you say, taken notice, it would appear that our task is infinitely more dangerous. We're out on the street there, exposed. I think I've seen a patrol car on that block only once since we started. You can't really expect us to go back under those circumstances.''

"That's right," Rena added with surprising firmness, taking another sip of tea with lemon to ease her tired vocal cords.

"What if I could arrange to get a policeman stationed on the block while we were there?'' Margaret asked. She looked around at her friends. "You know, a uniform and a gun—the whole thing. I don't think anyone would dare bother you. We could try it for a week, and it might be all we need.''

"I don't know," Sid said slowly. "It's still a little risky.''

"One week," Margaret said and held up a finger. "If nothing happens by Friday, we forget the whole thing.'' She looked directly at Thelma and Angelo sitting together at the far end of the table. "How about it?''

There was an extended silence punctuated now and then by the sound of clinking dishes at neighboring tables. No one wanted to talk. Finally, Angelo smiled awkwardly, felt reassuringly for the pistol in his pocket, and said, "Of course I'll continue. You've done this for our benefit," he said, with a glance at Thelma. "I can't even understand why all of you have gone this far.''

"Communal spirit," Sid said and laughed. "The community of retired meshugennahs. You can count me in, too. What's one more week of paranoia in the grand scheme of things? After all, this is New York.''

"Thanks, Sid," Margaret said.

"And me," said Thelma. "Anything's better than being homeless.''

"Okay," Bertie said reluctantly. "But just one week and only with the patrolman. Is that a deal?''

Margaret nodded.

"But how can you convince your police friend to get someone?" Bertie asked anxiously.

"Oh, I have my ways," Margaret said, winking. "Trust me."

Twenty-five

"ABSOLUTELY NOT," LIEUTENANT MORLEY said, trying to look sternly at Margaret. "Schaeffer's taking too much time off for you as it is. I can't keep him stationed on that block all day. And whatever the hell it is you're doing there, I want you to stop." He fixed Margaret with a stare that went right through her. "I can't have little old ladies getting stabbed in my precinct. Doesn't look good on the six o'clock news. You want to do something stupid like that, go crosstown to the Seventy-ninth Precinct and screw up their statistics." He looked over at Schaeffer and leaned back in his chair. "What about the knife?"

"A clean print, but so far we can't match it. Central computer kicked it out. No record with the FBI, the army, or downtown. Maybe the guy's just off the boat. The knife is your ordinary garden-variety switchblade. This one happened to have a five-inch blade." Schaeffer moved over next to Margaret and sat down. He put a hand on her arm and said softly, "Sam's right. Things are getting serious. Your two friends have been banged up. Next time—who knows what they'll do."

"No," Margaret said simply. She looked first at Schaeffer,

then at his boss. "We've gone this far, we're not giving up after our first confrontation. I've asked the others, and they agree. Maybe it'll take all nine of us on the block at one time. But so far what we're doing is working, and, as far as I know, there's no law that can keep law-abiding citizens from walking down a public street. I was hoping that from now on you might help us."

"The only way I can help you is by locking you up," Morley said. "You're all crazy, trying to go up against a guy like Farrell. He's probably got an unofficial city blessing. Come on, what's the point?"

"The point," Margaret said, stabbing out a cigarette, "is that Angelo Varonetti and Thelma Winters don't want to be told where to live by you, or by some manicured real-estate developer. They have little enough in savings and, unless they move away from all their friends in New York, they'd be facing the rest of their lives in tiny rooms in fleabag hotels. The point is that Farrell and his kind have gotten away with this too often in the past and, unless they are stopped somewhere, they'll continue to prey on the old people in this city. But the real point, I suppose, is that until you're old and alone you can't imagine how frightening it is to have the world turn its back on you—just like you're doing now." She sat back and glared at him, her face hot from excitement.

"Very stirring," Morley said. "I feel like I'm at a Gray Panther rally." He walked over to the window and silently traced his finger down a little crack in the right-hand sash.

"I came," Margaret repeated, "to get your help. I'm calling Farrell's bluff. I told his flunky that there'd be a policeman on the block. If it turns out that there are no police—" Margaret hesitated. "Well, then I suppose we're in for some real trouble. All it takes is one policeman, and I'm sure we can break Farrell down in a week or two." She got up and walked over behind Morley. "You see, Sam, it's really in your hands. We're going to continue with or without your help. Wouldn't it be better if you made things a little easier for us? I don't relish the idea of winding up in the hospital, you know."

Morley turned and faced her. There was a little struggle going on with the muscles of his mouth, but it looked like a little grin that was forming at the corners was winning out.

"You are, without a doubt, the most outrageous—"

Margaret held up a hand. "Save the compliments. Which is it to be? Do we get a policeman or not?"

Morley glanced in Schaeffer's direction and shrugged.

"Can we spare anyone for a couple of days?"

"I'll get Jacobson," Shaeffer said lightly. "It's an easy gig."

"Okay," Morley said. "Do it. But only for a week. After that, Margaret, I can't take the responsibility."

"Sam, you're a doll," Margaret said brightly. She stood on tiptoe and kissed Morley on the cheek. "I knew I could count on you." She turned and walked to the door. "We start at nine o'clock. See if you can have Jacobson there by a quarter of. You'll see—Farrell will topple like a house of cards."

Twenty-six

LUTHER PACED THE RUG IN FRONT OF Farrell's desk. There was still a soreness in his chest where he had hit the parking meter. But his most noticable souvenirs were his swollen lip and a thick gauze bandage which covered the puncture wound in his right hand. Farrell looked at him with disgust.

"Piece of cake, huh? Bunch of old winos. Whatsa' matter. Trip on your own shoelaces?"

"I'm going to kill her," Luther said softly. "No one does that to me and gets away with it. The bitch got lucky."

"Lucky or not, no one's going to do anything around here without my say-so. Now, sit down. You're making my neck hurt."

Luther eased himself into a salmon-colored corduroy chair in front of Farrell and took off his glasses. He rubbed the creases they had formed on the side of his face, then put them back on. After a few seconds his right leg started to vibrate up and down with nervous energy.

"Now listen to me and shut up," Farrell said. "Forget it. You carry out a little private vendetta and you'll find yourself on the streets again hustling dollar joints. There's a lot involved here. Everything's got to be thought out. I don't want you to blow everything with some bonehead play. You understand?"

Luther nodded slowly.

Farrell leaned back into the leather upholstery of his high-backed chair. "Now," he said. "Tell me what happened. I can see what they did to you. What did you do to them?"

Luther talked. Telling of the damage he'd done eased some of his anger. He gave an accurate description of everything up to and including his pursuit of Margaret. When he had finished, Farrell sat for over a minute with his eyes closed and his fingers pinching the bridge of his nose.

"Sounds like you got our point across," Farrell said finally. "Now we just wait and see if they heed the message. I think she was bluffing when she said they would continue and get a cop on the block." He shook his head. "Nah, you'll see. Tomorrow the block will be empty—no cops, no vagrants, nothing but customers. We ran a full-page ad in the *Times* today. Besides, the police aren't interested in a bunch of old hags. Just one thing—" he raised his chin a little. "What happened to the knife? When you started after her, you told me you pulled it. Then you told me she had you pinned with the fork." His eyebrow lifted.

"Musta dropped it when I fell."

"Fingerprints?"

"Suppose so. But I'm clean. I've never been printed."

"Well, then, it's all right," Farrell said softly and filed the information away in some little recess of his brain. "So now we wait."

"What if they're back?" Luther asked. "It's possible, ain't it?"

"If they're back?" Farrell shrugged. "I guess it will be time to take some other action, something more serious."

Luther grinned, and it made his bruised face look more sinister. "How serious?" he asked softly.

"Let's just say," Farrell nodded, "that you won't be disappointed." He held the other man's stare for a moment. Their silence was broken by the ring of the telephone. Luther reached over to answer it, and, after a moment, he covered the mouthpiece.

"Kravitz on the line—from L.A."

"Tell him I'm out."

Twenty-seven

THERE WAS PLENTY OF TRAFFIC. BY 10:30 A.M. Sid had counted no less than twenty prospective clients passing into Westhaven Tower. By 11:00, he sent Rena out for reinforcements, and by 11:30, all the condo killers, including Margaret, were working the block. Margaret had changed into some old sweaters and ripped stockings she kept in a rag pile. She huddled with Rose over one of the mid-block garbage cans and kept an eye on her chums. To her great relief, Jacobson was on the block. He was sitting inside a squad car a few yards away sipping coffee and watching with detached but amused interest the antics going on in front of him: Roosa weaved, Pancher politicked, Durso solicited, Rena sang, Bertie fed her pigeons, Rose and Margaret scavenged, Thelma called to her kitty, Sid touted, and Angelo panhandled. It was a zoo—all they lacked was a camera crew to make the seven o'clock news.

Along with Jacobson there was a second spectator, one who was not quite so amused. Luther, slumped down in the front seat of Farrell's Mercedes with an oversized pair of dark glasses and a gray felt hat covering much of his face, drove slowly down the block twice. The second time he double-parked at the end and watched in his rearview mirror. He took in Margaret and her nine friends and the police car and swore to himself. In half an hour he saw what they were doing to the market for luxury condominiums on West Ninety-third Street. People arrived on the block by foot and by taxi, but most fled before they reached Westhaven's door. He drove back to Farrell's office and reported. By that time, Farrell had already received confirmation from Mrs. Hart. The first question her few clients hit her with was whether it was always like that on the street. She was doing the best she could, but still no one had given her a deposit. By three o'clock that afternoon, Farrell had made up his mind. He sat down with Luther, disconnected his phones, and planned precisely how they would eliminate their problem.

"The little creep smokes, right?" Farrell asked.

"Like a chimney," Luther said.

"Good." Farrell smiled. "In fact, perfect."

Twenty-eight

THELMA BROUGHT THE NOTE SHE HAD found under her door to the strategy bench the next day. It was addressed to "Mrs. Freunglass" and said:

"It's about time we had another meeting in regard to our mutual interests. I have a proposition to make. Please call to set up an appointment. The number is 873-7351.
J. Farrell"

Margaret read the note a second time and a smile broke across her face. She passed it around to the others on the bench.

"That's it," she said. "He's giving up. See," she pointed. "A proposition to make."

The reactions of her friends were mixed. Their combined age of 700-plus years tempered their feelings with a certain skepticism. Pancher rubbed his narrow East European chin thoughtfully.

"Just like that?" he said.

"Why not," Margaret answered, lighting a Camel. "He knows when he's beaten. Did you see the way they were leaving yesterday?"

"Still," Sid slowly handed the note back. "You must be careful. Guys like that are most dangerous when they're losing."

Margaret inhaled deeply. "Of course I'll be careful," she said. "What do you think I am, a high school girl on my first

96

date? I'm not naive. He's not going to get any guarantee from us unless we get something in writing.''

Sid shook his head. ''I wasn't thinking about what kind of deal you're going to cut. I am more concerned with your safety. What if he wants to meet with you in his office?''

''Oh.'' Margaret stopped to think. ''You don't suppose—''

''I don't suppose anything. I just want you to be careful. In fact, I think if you've got to meet with him, you should meet with him here, where we can all keep an eye on you.'' Sid indicated the island on Broadway and the two large benches.

She shrugged. ''Let's see what he says first. I'd hate to hold up an agreement because we couldn't decide on where to meet.'' She looked at the number again and then stood up. ''Now,'' she said, ''Who's got a quarter?''

''Tavern on the Green,'' she said as she hung up. She turned out of the little phone booth and smiled at the friends, who stood waiting expectantly. ''Today at lunch. He's making reservations.''

''I don't like it,'' Durso said shaking his head.

''He suggested his office, I suggested Broadway.'' She shrugged. ''We compromised. Besides, I haven't had a swanky lunch in a long time.''

''But there are hundreds of restaurants on the West Side,'' Durso persisted. ''Why did he choose the only one that you have to get to through Central Park? I don't like it one bit.''

''Well,'' she said. ''In fact, he suggested he pick me up in his limousine, but I insisted on walking.'' She looked around innocently. ''Come on, there are a lot more people in the park than in his limousine.''

''Are you crazy!'' Sid exclaimed. ''I won't let you do it.''

''Now you listen to me, Mr. Rossman,'' Margaret said turning and glaring at him—''and you, too, all of you. I will not allow anyone to stop this meeting because of some silly worries. We've worked too hard to have it all fall apart because of something that is clearly illogical. What can he gain by harming me? Besides, the restaurant is a public place. There are a lot of people around." She hesitated for a moment. "And it's on the edge of the park. But, if it will make you feel any better, I don't suppose I'd mind if a couple of you went strolling uptown behind me." She looked back at Sid. "Okay?"

"Okay, but more than a couple," Sid said, looking down the bench. "Pancher, Roosa, Durso—that's four. We'll spread out. Two to the left, two to the right. The others can wait back here."

"Such a to-do," Margaret said, shaking her head. "You think it's necessary?"

"Absolutely," Bertie said. "Now what time are you meeting him?"

"One o'clock."

"That means you'll be finished around half-past one," Bertie said. "Be back here by two o'clock."

Margaret chuckled. "This is not lunch at your local ptomaine tearoom, dear. If you see me before three, I'll be surprised. In fact, I might even have a drink before we eat. That would be a nice way to begin a business lunch. Make that time half-past three."

"We'll be waiting," Sid said. "Don't worry."

Twenty-nine

MARGARET ARRIVED AT THE LARGE RES-taurant early and waited uneasily by the maitre d's mahogany reservations stand. As she watched, Gucci-belted mothers, wearing jeans by Calvin Klein, marched under the chandeliers with their young children; business-suited executives flashed gold tie clips and cuff links at each other; and elegant waiters bent solicitously to take their orders. There was an air of unreality to all of it. That such glitter should exist less than a few hundred yards from the old zoo's polar bear cage was hard to accept. The last time Margaret sat down for a meal in Central Park she had been overlooking the seal pond and eating from a brown paper bag.

She glanced obliquely at a menu nearby. Now what do you suppose a Belon oyster is, she wondered softly to herself.

"Hello, Mr. Farrell," the maitre d' said, beaming. "Your friend is right here." Margaret turned and saw the pin-striped suit and the paisley tie before she saw his face. There was still the same condescension in his features, including a grin that would have become a Rolls-Royce salesman. He nodded his head politely as he walked up, but his eyes studied her. His aftershave lotion preceded him by a good half second.

"Mrs. Freunglass," Farrell said, then turned abruptly to the maitre d'. "Where do you have us?"

"The crystal room today. This way please." Margaret followed the young man into a large room shimmering with gold tones, immaculate white tablecloths, and enough crystal hanging from the ceiling to dazzle an archduke. Their table was by the wall. From where she sat, Margaret could look out a window and reassure herself every now and then that they were still in Central Park, in the middle of Manhattan.

"Jack Daniels, straight up with a twist," Margaret said to the waiter when he came over. She settled back into the soft chair and picked up the menu.

"A martini, very dry," Farrell said and leaned forward. "I'm glad you decided to come," he added.

"Well, it's not for the company," she said sharply. "I'll just have the salade Niçoise and a little rye toast on the side." She reached into her handbag for a cigarette. Farrell had the lighter out by the time she put it into her mouth.

"Those things will kill you," he said as he snapped on the flame.

Margaret inhaled deeply. "That's what people have been

telling me for fifty-two years. I suppose it's going to catch up with me when I'm ninety.''

"You're optimistic,'' Farrell said. Soon the drinks arrived and Margaret was halfway down the Jack Daniels before Farrell spoke again.

"Don't misunderstand me,'' he began. "I like old people.''

"I know—some of them are your best parents.'' Margaret downed the rest of her drink.

"It's just that in this city, with space pushing two hundred dollars a square foot, it doesn't make economic sense to underutilize a convertible plot. As it is, I'm warehousing twenty empty apartments right now—twenty apartments— just so those two have a place to sleep at night.''

Margaret put her hand out. "Mr. Farrell, I'm not really interested in your problems. Prices per square foot are meaningless to me. The only thing I care about, quite simply, is seeing that my friends have a pleasant, affordable place to live. Besides, terms like 'underutilization' should be applied to machines, not people. I'm talking about lifetimes spent in one neighborhood, a network of friends, and patterns of living that are as much a part of them as their clothing. What does 'convertibility' have to do with that?'' She leaned back and allowed the waiter to put her salad down.

"You and your friends shouldn't be in New York,'' Farrell said. He picked up a knife and tapped it on the table. "When you get your golden kiss-off it means just that—go away. Go someplace where it's sunny—Florida or California. Some place like Carmel's got thousands of old people taking in the sun, and it never goes below seventy degrees all year. You've got to be crazy to want to stay around here.''

"Just a minute,'' Margaret interrupted. "I didn't come to get a travel lecture. I came because you mentioned something about a proposition. You're quite mistaken if you think I'll help you get my friends to leave. I'll be quite frank with you, the salade Niçoise is not that good to keep me here listening to your business problems. Actually, it's a bit salty if you ask me.'' She put a forkful in her mouth and made a face. "It's the anchovies.''

Farrell sighed. "Not even for cash?" He looked directly at her. "I mean to you."

"No." Margaret said it immediately. "If that's your proposition, then it's time for the bill."

"There's more," Farrell said and sighed. "But let's not spoil a perfectly good lunch. There's plenty of time to talk over dessert." He looked at his watch. "I don't have to be back to the office until three." He looked at the salad. "If you want to switch it, just say the word."

"It will do," Margaret said.

"Nice room," he said changing the subject. "I hear that Nancy Reagan was in the other day."

"I wouldn't know," Margaret said pointedly and speared a piece of lettuce with her fork.

By the time the dessert trolley rolled away, Margaret was becoming impatient to resume their negotiations. The last half-hour had been spent in talking about the unseasonably cool weather and the city budget deficit. Margaret was finishing her cup of tea when Farrell leaned forward and said abruptly, "Well, let's get back to business. All we have here is a little misunderstanding. I'm sure we can work something out."

"What did you have in mind?" Margaret said putting the cup down softly.

"Well, I thought perhaps Thelma Winters and Angelo Varonetti would like some money. Say ten thousand dollars each. I have it waiting in my office."

"I'm afraid that won't do." Margaret looked at him steadily. "There was a point when Varonetti might have accepted a reasonable cash payment. Now, however, after your hired thug broke his foot, he's not interested in moving for any amount. Among other things, it's a matter of pride. He comes from the old school. Yes, and I'm afraid that Mrs. Winters feels quite the same way." She shook her head. "No point in offering money now, it's too late." She pulled out another cigarette and lit it herself. "No, Mr. Farrell, here's the only proposition you can make that's acceptable to us. First, all harassment must stop immediately. Second, we want a signed, notarized statement from you confessing to all the past harassment of the tenants at 621 West Ninety-first Street. We will not use this document against you unless new incidents occur. Third, we want an escrow account of ten thousand dollars established to pay for heating oil and maintenance. Anything left over at the end of the year will be credited to the next year's escrow account. And finally,'' Margaret stopped for a puff on her cigarette, ''Mr. Varonetti wants $492 for reimbursement of medical costs incurred with his fractured metatarsal. As soon as you comply with these things, we will stop our operations on West Ninety-third Street, which, as I'm sure you know, have been rather effective.'' She smiled politely. ''You're right,'' she added. ''It's really quite simple. Just a little misunderstanding.'' She took another puff of her cigarette and stabbed it out. ''I wonder if I could get a little more tea?''

Farrell didn't move for a few seconds, then turned and signaled to the waiter.

''A confession?'' he said after the young man had scurried off for the tea.

''Notarized,'' Margaret added. ''I'm sure you understand the need for such a document given your record.''

There was another long silence while Farrell studied her.

''How do I know you won't use it?'' he asked finally.

''You don't,'' Margaret said. ''Just like Thelma won't know if her foot's next. Oh, thank you,'' she said as the fresh tea bag arrived on her saucer.

Farrell looked at his watch. ''All right,'' he said slowly. ''It's getting late. Why don't we walk back to my office. If there is anything specific you want me to say, you can tell me on the way.''

''Yes, there are some specifics. I suppose we could begin with the cockroaches.'' Margaret looked down wistfully at the fresh teabag, then in one quick motion, grabbed it and put it in her handbag. ''Pity to waste it,'' she said dabbing at her mouth with a napkin.

Farrell paid, slipped the maitre d' a five-dollar bill on the way out, then led Margaret through the front door.

"Ah, fresh air," she said. "It's a wonder there's any left in New York. Which way, Mr. Farrell?"

"This direction. It's so much nicer through the park. It brings us right out at Seventy-second Street." He set off over the grass with Margaret keeping pace with him. "Why not?" she thought. Her friends were close behind. It was 2:45 by her watch.

Sid and Durso, standing in front of one of the large sycamore trees nearby watched as Margaret and Farrell moved away. Sid motioned to Pancher about thirty yards away and they all stepped out. The route they were taking paralleled the bridle path. It was much more secluded than the normal pedestrian route that followed the car roadway. Occasionally someone in jodhpurs and a pinched-waist tweed coat trotted by on a horse, but all the bicyclists and skaters skimmed by up on the asphalt. Farrell kept up a steady pace, commenting on a few of the several points Margaret was voicing. Only once did he look back, but he showed no surprise when he saw the four old men tagging along several yards behind. They made no attempt to conceal themselves. Their plan was to dissuade rather than to intervene. They never got closer than fifteen yards, and they kept up a constant chatter. It took more than ten minutes for the members of the little procession to exit from the park. When they did, they made a right turn and continued walking north on Central Park West. Pancher breathed a little more easily when they were back on the city streets. A few more minutes brought them in front of Farrell's Central Park West address.

"Thank you for the lunch," Margaret said. "Quite unnecessary, really. We could have had our talk on one of these park benches."

Farrell took one last look behind him. "I almost feel we have," he said.

"Still," she smiled. "It was a nice little treat. And I'm so glad you've decided to be reasonable about this whole matter. You will have that paper for me tomorrow with all those things I mentioned?"

"Tomorrow," he repeated. "Why don't you come by with

Mr. Varonetti and Mrs. Winters. I'd like to make my apologies in person. Oh, yes.'' He hesitated. "And after tomorrow let's have no more trouble on West Ninety-third Street. You understand.''

"Understand?'' Margaret repeated with a puzzled expression, but Farrell had turned and was walking into his building. As Margaret watched him, her four friends came up behind her.

"Everything go all right?'' Sid asked.

"I think so,'' Margaret answered slowly. She shook her head. "It was all so easy—almost too easy.''

"The money, too?'' Durso asked.

Margaret nodded and a little frown wrinkled her forehead. "Where're Thelma and Angelo?'' she asked.

The four men looked at each other. "I think Thelma was going shopping this morning,'' Roosa said. "Angelo was going to stay on Ninety-third Street with the others.''

"No, wait a minute,'' Sid interrupted. "He said something about going home for his Social Security check—he needed to cash it right away. He usually goes home for his mail around one o'clock.''

Thirty

ANGELO ARRIVED HOME THAT AFTERNOON at precisely one o'clock, so intent on retrieving his Social Security check that he failed to notice the little irregularity above the outside door. Tacked to the frame, was the end of a six-inch section of lightweight hardware-store chain. The other end was stretched horizontally and was held in place by a length of tape that ran vertically to the front door. It was the simplest of devices, one Luther had learned when he was fifteen. Angelo inserted his key and opened the door. The tape pulled away and the chain dropped. When the door closed behind Angelo, the sandwiched chain kept it slightly ajar. Luther smirked to himself as he walked up the entrance steps two minutes later. He carefully removed the tape, still attached to the door, and pulled the tack and chain away. He slipped quickly into the vestibule and waited while his eyes adjusted to the dim light. The first thing he saw was the "out of order" sign on the elevator. Then he heard Angelo's footsteps on the staircase, the telltale clumping of a man walking with an unwieldy cast. The noise stopped and Luther flattened himself against the wall.

"Who's that?" Angelo asked. "Anybody there?" There was silence for another thirty seconds as Angelo tried to make sense out of the noise he had heard and the tiny draft of air.

"Thelma?" he called again and took a few tentative steps back down the staircase. When he looked into the dim vestibule he saw nothing. He took a deep breath and turned back upstairs. There was a time, he remembered, when the stairwell had been full of noise, and when the halls smelled of Mrs. Pearle's pot roasts or Mrs. Ramey's baking. Now there was only a chalky smell that stuck to your clothes and stayed with you for several blocks outside.

"A morgue," Angelo said, coughing.

Luther waited until he heard Angelo step on the first landing, then crept up after him. He could have taken the old man anytime, but Farrell had said to make it look natural. So Luther waited again at the top while Angelo opened his door and passed through. Then, as quickly as he could, he rushed for the closing door. He barely managed to get a foot in the jamb and keep it open. Angelo was midway into the room and as he whirled around, Luther could see the envelope in his hand. He slowly closed the door behind him and grinned.

"Remember me?"

The expression on the older man's face was a mixture of

surprise and fear. His eyes closed into narrow slits, but his lower lip trembled softly.

"You won't be getting any more mail where you're going, Pop," Luther said. "Should'a taken that ticket and gone down to Baltimore." Slowly he reached into his trouser pocket and withdrew a crumpled black plastic garbage bag. "Should'a left New York." He took a step forward.

Angelo dropped the envelope and shoved his hand into his coat pocket.

"Don't come any closer. I've got a gun."

Luther laughed. It was a sound full of impudence and cruelty. "Sure, old man. All those TV movies have gone to your head. Sorry, but this ain't a sitcom." He took another step.

The room exploded with the noise and Luther felt a pain in his leg.

"Son-of-a-bitch!" he yelled and pitched forward. He kept himself from falling to the floor by grabbing onto a little glass-topped coffee table. When he looked up again, he saw the wisp of smoke coming out of the neat little hole in Angelo's jacket. The old man was also staring down at his pocket with almost as much surprise. Luther stood up and took a halting step backward.

"Stand still," Angelo said. "I'm calling the cops." As the older man reached for the phone, Luther did something so instinctual, he couldn't stop himself. He took another step backwards and turned to run.

"Hold it!"

In the deadly silence that filled the room, they both heard the muffled click of the gun as the hammer wedged down on a fold of fabric in Angelo's pocket. Luther stopped and faced Angelo again. For a split second, his features twisted into a triumphant sneer, and then he lunged off his good leg. His palm caught Angelo in the rib cage and knocked the wind out of him. Angelo slumped to the floor gasping for breath.

"Little creep," Luther said, bending down to retrieve the black plastic bag. Unceremoniously he slipped it over Angelo's head and closed it off at the neck with a broad rubber band. Then he sat down behind the older man and held tightly onto both of his hands. They remained that way for ten minutes. For the first five minutes Angelo continued to move. His body jerked back and forth, trying desperately to fight the bag off his head. Slowly his movements became more intermittent until he lay absolutely still. Luther held on a little longer, then got up and removed the bag. He massaged Angelo's neck for a minute to take away the light mark of the rubber band, then felt for a pulse. There was none. He lay face up on the linoleum with his eyes wide open. Luther made sure to close the lids, as Farrell had instructed, then took care of his own wound. The bullet had grazed his thigh three inches above the knee. He made a bandage out of one of Angelo's shirts, then washed what little blood there was off the floor. Next, he removed the coat Angelo was wearing and hung it back up in the closet with the gun still inside. The old man was heavy, but he lifted him onto his bed. He undid the laces and placed the old wing tips neatly at the foot of the bed. Then he lit a cigarette he found on the night table, puffed a few times, and laid it down on the bed next to Angelo's inert hand. As he watched, the blanket began to char, then smoulder. When a steady stream of white smoke started rising he turned and made his exit. He was careful to touch the doorknob with a handkerchief he had brought with him. Before he closed the door, he took a last look at the scene. Nothing out of the ordinary. A poor old man dead from smoke inhalation. Happens all the time. Closing the door, Luther consulted his watch—2:15 P.M.—perfect. He walked back down the stairs and stopped at Thelma's door. One down, one to go. He listened carefully at the door to make sure no one was at home. After a minute, he started in on the lock. It was one of the older cylinder types and in no time he was inside the apartment. He went immediately to the bathroom, found what he was looking for, and did what Farrell had instructed. Then he left quickly. The smell of smoke was already in the downstairs vestibule when he slipped out onto the street. The Mercedes was just around the corner and he got to it without passing anyone. He could have waited for the fire engines to make sure, but he figured that would take at least another half-hour. By then he could be washed up and bandaged properly.

"Little creep," he said again. "Who would have thought he'd have a gun?" He started the motor. "Farrell will be pleased," he thought. "Everything according to plan." He looked down at the bulge under his trouser leg and cursed. "Almost everything. That's going to hurt like hell tomorrow."

Thirty-one

THE FIRE ENGINES ARRIVED AT 3:10 P.M., three minutes after the first call. By then smoke was pouring out of the third-floor apartment thickly enough to rise seven stories in a congealed column before dissipating over the roofs of nearby buildings. It was a cold fire, the firemen noticed when they finally thrust their way into Angelo's room—no oil, grease, or rubber. Just an old mattress, dirty rug, and enough smoke to keep them choking for several minutes. Peering through the acrid haze, they found the old man's body on the charred bed. The matches and pack of cigarettes that had obviously caused the fire lay undamaged on the night table. The fire chief shook his head as he watched them pack the body bag and remove the victim.

"Another jerk asleep with a lighted cigarette," he said, looking around the small apartment and picking out the three ashtrays full of cigarettes. "They want to kill themselves, but I just wish they wouldn't do it on my shift." He shouted something else to his assistant and took a last look around. "Goddamn it," he said, tramping out of the apartment and down through the empty building. On the street, a large knot of people stood in a semi-circle outside the radius of the trucks. Murmuring and questioning one another, they gazed up at the spreading black stain on the building wall. Some of them pointed, several gasped when the body was removed, and one older woman with dyed red hair and a bag full of groceries remained so immobile and unblinking that a few of those nearby wondered if she might be blind. But Thelma was in a state of near shock. Slowly she set the bag down on the sidewalk and leaned against a car for support.

"Something wrong, lady?" one of the kids watching said maliciously. "Never seen a dead body before?"

Thelma let out a squeal of pain so piercing that almost everyone turned away from the building to look at her. She ran over to the ambulance and put a hand on the stretcher.

"They killed him," she said in a whisper. "My God, they've killed him."

One of the ambulance attendants walked up to her side.

"You knew him?"

"There was just the two of us left," she said and the tears finally began to well up in her eyes.

"You better come with us," the attendant said. "We'll need some information." He closed the back doors and led her to the front. She got in without another word.

Thirty-two

FARRELL WAS IN A FINE RAGE AND DOING his best not to show it. Luther sat before him on the couch with his leg propped up, a clean gauze bandage applied to the wound. There was a look of mild confusion on his face like that of a little child who has been told that his crayoning of the couch is not acceptable.

"Well, apart from this," he gestured to his leg, "I thought it went down perfectly. You got your alibi at that restaurant and one less tenant. After what I did in the old lady's apartment, you'll soon have no tenants. There's no way they're gonna figure it other than the way you said. The place was clean when I left—no trace of nothing."

"What about the bullet?" Farrell asked tightly. "It's not in your leg."

"In the wall somewhere. But the place has such chipped and peeling paint no one'd ever spot it."

"Sure. And the blood?"

"Washed it away."

Farrell mused aloud. "I don't like it—maybe someone heard the shot."

"Ha," Luther laughed. "Ease up, boss. Like I said, no problems—not even in the old lady's apartment. When I left there wasn't a soul on the street."

Farrell leaned back. "What happened after you got hit?"

Luther looked impatient. "Like I told you, I lunged for him. I was careful not to hit him in the face."

"You didn't fall or anything? Maybe touch something?"

Luther's face clouded over. A frown creased his forehead. "Well, hell, maybe I stumbled. Who knows?"

"Grabbed onto something?"

Luther shifted uneasily. "I could have. There was a little table there."

A slight change came over Farrell's face, and he sat upright.

"Yeah, it probably doesn't matter. They won't be looking for prints." He got up and walked over behind him. "You did a good job, Luther. I'm proud of you. What do you say we celebrate tonight? You know that restaurant you took Kravitz and me to over in Long Island City a coupla months ago?"

"One with the Lobster Diavalo?"

"That's the one. What do you say we go again? Just the two of us."

"Sure, boss," Luther said. "What time?"

"Say about nine. It's always crowded earlier."

Luther stood up shakily and steadied himself against the wall. "Maybe I better go and lie down. This thing's really starting to hurt."

"Yeah, do that," Farrell said. "See you later." He watched intently as Luther headed out the door.

Thirty-three

MORLEY RUBBED HIS EYES AS THOUGH HE were trying to clear them of sleep. It was too early to have to deal with all of this. Death was horrible enough, it was worse before his morning coffee. He blinked and put on his glasses. They were still there—Margaret and two of her Broadway friends, Thelma and Sid. From time to time, Thelma pressed a handkerchief to her face, and Sid was looking serious to the point of ignoring copies of *The Racing Form* on a nearby table. Schaeffer stood over the three of them like an attorney for the defense.

"Listen," he said in a weary voice. "The report I got from the fire marshal had it as an accidental death from smoking in bed—no signs of arson, chemicals, or forced entry. They treated it routinely; there are a hundred similar accidents a year." Morley raised a hand. "I know what you're going to say and I'm way ahead of you. I had the coroner's office do a postmortem examination." He leaned back in his chair.

"There's no doubt he was murdered. Death was by suffocation, not by smoke inhalation. So then I asked Schaeffer to go back and check the apartment yesterday afternoon with a crime-scene unit. There's a bullet embedded in the wall which must have lodged there yesterday because there's a trace of fresh blood on it. Schaeffer's good at spotting little details. But it wasn't Varonetti's blood. He must have clipped his murderer below the waist from the position of the hole on the wall."

"He had a gun?" Margaret asked, surprised.

Morley opened a drawer and pulled out the little revolver. He laid it on the desk. "Schaeffer found it in the pocket of one of the jackets in the closet. There's a hole in the fabric where the bullet passed through. I asked the medical examiner to double-check and, sure enough, there was cordite on Varonetti's right hand. As you can see, this is not adding up to accidental death." He lifted the gun and turned it over. "We're tracing it now. For some reason," he smiled, "it's still got its numbers on it."

"But it wasn't the murderer's," Schaeffer added. "If he went to all the trouble of hanging up Angelo's coat after he killed him, he would have taken his gun back."

"Still, it's a lead," Morley said.

"Lead!" Margaret frowned. "But surely you know who killed him—Farrell."

Morley looked pained. "Varonetti died at two o'clock, give or take a quarter of an hour," he said. "Yesterday, between one and three o'clock, Farrell was with you at Tavern on the Green—on your own admission. He said 'hello' to the maitre d' when he came in and tipped him when he left." Morley shook his head. "Try again."

"You know what I mean, Sam. If it wasn't Farrell, it was his hired thug. No one else had a motive."

"You don't bring cases before the grand jury on motive. You need hard evidence."

"What further evidence do you need? Farrell's been harassing people in that building for years."

"Maybe Mantex has," Morley said. "But linking up Farrell to Mantex is another matter. My bet is he gets other people to do his dirty work, people who may not even know who he is.''

''Geraldo,'' Thelma said.

''Yeah, maybe, but not for Angelo's death,'' Schaeffer said. ''I've already checked and yesterday he was repairing a refrigerator in the other building where he works. He was there from a little after 1:00 P.M. until 3:30. The woman whose fridge it was swears he didn't leave except once for less than a minute to get a different tool. That's not enough time to walk two blocks and kill someone.''

Margaret lit the cigarette angrily and fired the match into the wastebasket.

''So you're telling me there's nothing you can do. Angelo is dead, I feel as guilty as hell, and you're going to sit on your hands.''

There was silence in the room.

''Tell her about the print,'' Schaeffer said.

''What print?'' Margaret asked.

''Varonetti's apartment had a set of fingerprints that didn't match up with anything else. They were found on the coffee table, the kind of print you'd get if someone grabbed the table to keep himself from falling.'' He let that sink in for a few seconds. ''We ran it through our records and came up with nothing. Then this morning Schaeffer had an idea. We checked it against the knife that guy pulled on you—they match up perfectly. But we're not home yet.'' Morley got up and paced to the window. ''First of all, we've got to find him, second, we have to prove he was Farrell's flunky, and third, if you want Farrell, you got to convince this guy to cop a plea and implicate his boss. It's not cut-and-dry, but we've got a pretty good start.'' He went back to his desk and sat down. ''We can match his blood type with that on the bullet as another piece of hard evidence.''

''And I can testify that I saw him in Farrell's office,'' Margaret said. ''I did, too—that day I went to talk to him. That will establish the connection.''

''Good.'' Morley leaned back. ''Personally, I think we'll get him. If it hadn't been for the gun, they might have pulled it off. Let's hope they still think they did. Nothing's going out to the press to change that impression. Varonetti's death is still listed as accidental.'' He smiled thinly. ''With any luck we'll pick him up by evening—somewhere near Farrell's apartment.''

Margaret nodded. She turned sideways and looked at her friends sitting next to her. ''What about Thelma? Certainly she can't stay in that building all alone.''

''Until Farrell's behind bars, I don't think I'd let her out of my sight,'' Schaeffer said. ''She's the only one that stands in his way now. She goes, and the building is his to tear down.''

''As long as she continues to pay her rent every month she's protected,'' Morley said. ''But no question about it, she's got to get out.'' Everyone looked at Thelma. ''Mrs. Winters, have you anywhere to go?''

Thelma's eyes opened wide. ''No, I haven't slept anywhere but in my own bed for the past forty-two years. I wouldn't know where to go now.''

''But that's easy,'' Margaret said. ''With me. I have plenty of room.''

Thelma shook her head. ''I couldn't.''

''Nonsense,'' Margaret insisted. ''It's settled. I'll go back with you this morning, and you'll throw some things together. When Farrell is taken care of, you can return. Maybe David could go back with us.'' Margaret stopped, overcome with sadness. ''Angelo was such a nice man,'' she said. ''I do feel terribly guilty—it's my fault that things happened the way they did.''

''You couldn't know,'' Sid said gently. ''We were all just trying to help. Who knew they'd go that far?''

''I should have,'' she said. ''I'm responsible.''

The phone rang on Morley's desk. Margaret moved to the door and waited until Sid and Thelma followed. Schaeffer had his hand on the knob when Morley raised his voice.

''Hold it.''

They all turned to watch him. The expression on his face revealed nothing.

''Was there another bullet wound?'' Schaeffer walked back

over to the desk. He watched as Morley wrote something down. "Thanks, Jim." Morley hung up the phone softly.

"Murphey down at the morgue?" Schaeffer asked apprehensively.

Morley nodded. "He always calls up with any unidentified stiff north of Fifty-ninth Street." He tapped the pad he had been scribbling on. "This one floated to shore about two hours ago near Gracie Mansion. Gunshot wound at the base of the skull." Morley lit a cigarette angrily. "Another bullet wound in the thigh, older because it had a bandage on it. He was a six-foot man, heavy-set, and in his late thirties," Morley continued. "With marks on his temples from tight glasses—"

"You think—?" Margaret began.

"Yeah, why not? It makes sense. Now Farrell's covered."

"He's very clever, Sam. It's going to be hard to outsmart him."

"Leave that to us," Morley said.

Schaeffer excused himself and went to a room two doors away where a man was on the phone. Schaeffer waited until he was free. They talked for a minute, then Schaeffer wrote something down. When he came back to the little group by the door, he looked puzzled.

"Looks like Angelo had a friend in low places. The gun belonged to a guy named Donghia, an old petty mafioso who runs a bakery down in the village. Staunton's going down now to ask him some questions." He held the door open for Margaret, Thelma, and Sid. "Too bad he didn't give Angelo target practice to go along with the gun."

"Donghia?" Margaret asked when they reached the street.

"You know him?" Sid asked curiously.

"No, not yet."

Thirty-four

       MARGARET WAS INTOXICATED WITH THE smell before she reached the second-floor landing. Donghia had told her the address on Carmine Street, but he hadn't mentioned anything about the bakery downstairs. She continued up the staircase, taking in the aroma of baking bread that was rising with her. At Donghia's door she paused only long enough to adjust the little felt hat on her head before she knocked. The door was opened by an old gentleman with white hair and a careful smile. Very politely, he ushered Margaret into the living room and then sat down next to her.

"On the phone," Donghia began, "you mentioned that you were a friend of Angelo's. It's a tragedy. He was a good man, a proud man, but he should have given up those lousy cigarettes. What a way to go." He shook his head. "Can I get you something? A cannoli, maybe—light as a feather."

"No, thank you." Margaret smiled and looked around the room. Every available surface had something on it—little carved china figurines, brass clocks, paperweights. The walls were equally crowded with paintings, most of them of a religious nature. There were slipcovers on the furniture and a polished linoleum floor covered by a few scatter rugs in the living room.

"I would like some tea," she said finally. "No sugar."

Donghia called into the kitchen in Italian, then leaned back and gave Margaret an appraising glance. "So you were a friend of Angelo's?" he repeated. "Very nice for both of you."

"The gun," Margaret said slowly. "They asked you about it?"

Donghia's eyes flickered for an instant. "This afternoon they came." He shrugged. "I told them what happened when Angelo was here to see me. I suppose I should have denied Angelo his request, but it was the only favor he ever asked. I'm glad that he didn't use it."

"Oh, but he did," Margaret said. "Unfortunately, he didn't aim well. The police are keeping things quiet, but you might as well know. Especially since I'm going to need your help." She smiled at the young woman who brought in the cup of tea.

"My daughter," Donghia said.

Margaret nodded at her. "Perhaps I will have the cannoli after all—it's a long story." She took a sip of the tea, then sat back again. "Angelo was murdered," she announced, looking straight at Donghia. "By a man named Jason Farrell." She started from the beginning and told Donghia everything. "I came to you because you were his friend," Margaret concluded, "the person he came to when he needed help." She looked around. "You understand this is a bit unusual for me. I'm somewhat out of my element. I don't really know how to ask this—"

"If I understand you correctly, you want me to ah—avenge Angelo's death. Just because I gave him the gun, you think maybe I'm in the business."

Margaret reddened. "Good heavens, no. That's not what I had in mind at all."

"Oh?" Donghia smiled.

Margaret cleared her throat. "No, it's something else," she said. "A few phone calls out to the West Coast that's all. You must have friends there?"

"I have friends all over," Donghia said evenly. "That's how I stay in business. California—" He nodded. "Where?"

"Carmel," Margaret answered. "It's something that just popped into my head this afternoon."

"You tell me what it is you want," Donghia said, "and I'll do my best to get it. I knew Angelo for a long time. What about Carmel?"

"A company called Financial Diversified Industries," Margaret said. Donghia reached for a pen and wrote it down. "They're somehow involved in this project that Farrell is behind. I think it's called Mayberry Mews. They're loaning him a lot of money in a peculiar kind of mortgage that converts to an equity position. Do you know about real estate?"

Donghia shook his head, no.

"Then at that lunch we had, Farrell mentioned Carmel. It passed right over me until I thought about it. Of all the warm, sunny places he could have mentioned for us old-timers to go, why Carmel? Why not Palm Springs or Albuquerque?" She smoothed out her dress. "It's because Carmel was on his mind, and I'd like to know why."

"Percippio is out near there," Donghia said. "Yeah, I think he's in L.A. That's near enough."

"The company, the people, the deal if possible. Anything you can get," Margaret said. "I'd appreciate it."

"Give me a week," Donghia said. "That should be enough. I'll call. You got a number?"

Margaret gave it to him and stood up. "You've been very kind. It's no wonder that Angelo came to see you."

Donghia saw her to the door. "If you liked the cannoli, come again. They come from downstairs—my own bakery."

Margaret smiled. "You'll have to come and try my schnecken some day."

Donghia bowed. "It would be a real pleasure," he said and closed the door softly.

Thirty-five

MARGARET HAD NEVER REMOVED THE second twin bed in her apartment after Oscar died. The one time she had seriously thought of removing it she had insomnia for three nights. It stayed where it was and functioned interchangeably as a horizontal wardrobe, a staging area for her knitting projects, and a magazine and book rack. For Thelma's visit, all these objects had been cleared off to make room for a fresh set of linens and the afghan comforter that Margaret had won in the Florence K. Bliss raffle three years earlier.

"Won't this be fun?" Margaret said as they arranged the bathroom so that there would be no confusion over toothbrushes or shampoos.

Thelma tried to respond cheerfully, but she found it difficult. Later that first day, when Margaret was dusting the bookshelves, Thelma sat down on the couch and cried softly. Margaret put her arm around her.

"I was thinking," Thelma sniffed, "about Angelo."

They developed a routine that took Thelma's mind off her troubles. They took their breakfasts together, which they finished at 8:15 A.M. Next was the daily crossword puzzle, which they usually completed by 9:30 before going out. Every other day they went grocery shopping. If the weather was fine, lunch was a couple of sandwiches and a thermos of tea on the Eighty-second Street bench. In the afternoons, every afternoon, they went to the Bliss Center for their day's so-

cializing. Never once was Thelma left alone. The only con-
cession they made to their protected existence was to cancel
any activity that took place at night. In place of bingo, they
played gin rummy on Margaret's dining-room table, the front
door double-locked and chained. Thelma was always the last
to go to bed, invariably at least a half-hour after Margaret
had put down the mystery book she was reading and turned
out her bedside lamp. At the end of the week, Thelma sent
her check to Mantex and they waited for news from Schaeffer.

A few days later they saw Schaeffer crossing the street
toward their bench. The weather had turned hot enough for
his old UCLA tee shirt. His beard looked like it hadn't been
combed in a week.

"How's it going?" he asked nonchalantly, sitting down
next to Margaret.

"So?" demanded Margaret. "We've been waiting all week
for news."

Schaeffer shifted. "Precisely nothing. I can tell you what
we've tried, but it all boils down to the same thing. Farrell's
always one step ahead."

"Go ahead, we're listening."

"Well, first of all, we've got a tail on him. So far he's as
clean as Snow White. He hasn't met with anybody suspi-
cious, in fact, he rarely goes out—lunch twice, all alone at a
fancy place on Columbus. Morley's pulling the tail as of this
afternoon. Two hundred man-hour's worth of occasional lun-
cheon reports is not, as they say downtown, cost-efficient."

Margaret grumbled. "What about confirming that the man
who killed Angelo worked for him?"

"He's ahead of us on that one, too. Staunton spoke to the
doorman where Farrell lives. He didn't know anything. When
he saw the guy's picture, Staunton said he stiffened like he'd
been varnished. Still nothing. Money talks and Farrell's got
enough to shout his way out of trouble."

"It's not fair," Thelma said.

"Yeah, what else is new?" Schaeffer said. He squinted at

Thelma as she put a hand suddenly to her stomach. "Whatsa' matter, I say something you didn't know?"

Thelma took her hand away. "No, just a little gas. I get it now and then."

"Nothing else linking Farrell to Angelo's death?" Margaret asked.

"I spoke to Geraldo at Mrs. Winters's building."

"And?"

"—Like talking to a lemon that's been in the fridge too long," Schaeffer said. "Cold, sour, and sick-looking. Told me he didn't know anybody by the name of Farrell. The only guy he knew in regard to the building was called Moore. He called him 'Mr. M' for short."

"That's who he mentioned when Sid was there," Margaret said.

"Moore may be Farrell," Schaeffer pointed out, "but it doesn't matter because Geraldo has never seen him."

"But what about Geraldo's salary and checks?" Thelma asked. "Wasn't there a signature?"

"Listen to this," Schaeffer said. "Geraldo got paid every week in cash. He liked that a lot because it was off the books. The money was delivered to him by a big guy with dark hair and glasses that were too tight. I showed him the picture and he said that that was the guy. Funny, huh? We can make the link from Mantex to the killer, but we can't make the link from the killer to Farrell."

"The phone," Margaret insisted. "He had the number on his desk."

"Yes, the phone." Schaeffer shook his head. "I asked Geraldo how he got in touch with Moore when he needed something, like money for supplies. He said he told the guy that paid him. 'No phone number?' I asked. He gave me the blankest look since Nixon was asked about Watergate. And the desk," Schaeffer shook his head, "had just been painted. Geraldo's bought and we're on the outside looking in."

Thirty-six

THAT NIGHT THE GIN RUMMY GAME WAS halted after ten minutes because of Thelma's stomach.

"You better lie down," Margaret said. "Perhaps we should call a doctor."

"I hate doctors. All they do is jab and poke at you and then tell you you're fine. I'll be all right in the morning. Something I ate must have disagreed with me."

"But Thelma, we ate the same things," Margaret said.

"That's why there's no need to worry. I know what you're thinking."

Margaret shook her head. "Still, how long have you felt this way?"

Thelma thought for a minute. "About two days."

"Two days!" Margaret frowned. "And you didn't say anything."

"It wasn't anything yesterday. Today it's only a little worse. But I think it's going away now. Just let me rest." She closed her eyes, and in two minutes she was snoring.

Margaret went to the kitchen and opened the refrigerator. She lifted out a half-open container of milk, hesitated for a moment, then with a shrug poured it into the sink. Methodically, she took the other opened containers and threw them away. "Tomorrow we start fresh." She was looking for her cigarettes when the telephone rang.

"Mrs. Binton," came the soft, accented voice.

122

"Yes?"

"It's Donghia. I've got something for you."

Thirty-seven

THE MUSEUM CAFÉ AT WEST SEVENTY-seventh Street was never crowded at 11:30 A.M. when it opened. Margaret saw him sitting at the little table by the window even before she entered the restaurant. Donghia looked very formal in a wide-shouldered suit and dark-blue tie.

"Thank you," Margaret said as she sat down, "for coming all the way uptown."

Donghia grinned. "The last time I came up to the West Side, Basilio outpointed Gaspar Ortega in ten rounds at the old Garden. I'm having steak and eggs. You want some?"

Margaret shook her head. She reached into her bag for her cigarettes, lit one carefully, then leaned forward. "What did you find out?"

"As I told you, Joe Percippio's out in L.A. and has been there long enough to have a nice little network—'Fingers' he calls them. He's got these stores all over that rent his video machines. Merchants need his machines, so all he has to do is sneeze and favors come rolling in. One question and the man in Carmel worked up a sweat tracking it down. It seems his brother knows somebody who works for a guy named Manny Kravitz." Donghia took a swallow of coffee and cleared space for the plate of eggs that arrived. "You sure?" he offered, pointing to the food.

"No, thank you. Go ahead."

"This guy, Kravitz, is kind of a renegade real-estate mogul. Made his bones back in Texas in little shopping arcades. I think there are some bodies along the way, but don't quote me. Anyway, once he moved out to California, he started getting bigger—malls and swingers' high-rises. Pretty successful. He's got construction going on in Chicago, Alaska, and Georgia. But everything's always legal now—he gets the others to do any dirty work."

Margaret stopped him. "Kravitz is involved with this Financial Diversified Industries?"

"Kravitz *is* Financial Diversified Industries," Donghia said. "All twenty-five million dollars of its net worth." He smiled at Margaret's reaction. "Which is not bad for a little boy from Austin." He finished his eggs and sat back. "Which brings us to Jason Farrell. Farrell, it seems, doesn't mind doing dirty work—it was a match made in heaven." Donghia chuckled. "Sometimes I wonder why I don't branch out like these guys. There's a whole world out there just waiting for me."

"Stick to your cannoli," Margaret said. "Now, what's this Mayflower Mews?"

"Mayberry Mews," Donghia corrected, "is supposed to be a commercial development to rival the biggest in the city—five-hundred-unit residential, plus 25,000 square feet of stores. Kravitz put up five hundred thousand dollars of seed money in the form of a mortgage on Angelo's building. The whole project was held up because of the tenancy in the building. That's why Kravitz gave himself an out—he gave Farrell three years to clear the buildings. If the people were out, Kravitz would come up with another million and a half and become a fifteen-percent partner."

"But if there were still tenants left after three years?" Margaret asked.

"He'd take back his mortgage and leave Farrell high and dry. There'd be architectural fees to pay as well as other expenses. Farrell would take a bath."

"But what if he just defaulted on the mortgage?" she asked.

"The way I understand it," Donghia said slowly, "you don't do things like that to Kravitz." He made his fingers into a mock pistol and pulled the trigger.

"Oh," Margaret said. Her cigarette was waiting for her in the ashtray and she took another puff. "And when," she asked hesitantly, "is the three years over?"

"On September 21," Donghia said. "Two weeks away, and Percippio's man said Kravitz is on top of it."

"Just as I thought," Margaret said to herself and stabbed out the cigarette. "Thelma's in real trouble."

Donghia heard. "Who's Thelma?"

"The last registered tenant in the building. She's staying with me for safety." Margaret looked at him nervously. "What do you think?"

Donghia shook his head. "Why don't you get out of town? It's only for two weeks."

"Yes, I'm sure that's the best idea," Margaret said. "Except that she doesn't have a relative she can pop in on or money enough for travel and hotels. We'll have to stay around here and make sure she's never alone."

Donghia lifted his eyes. "If she stays around here, she's dead. Now listen to me." He put a hand on Margaret's arm. "My niece Natalie and her husband run this little guest house up in Leeds in the Catskills—rooms for rent and a small dining-room for meals. They do most of their business in the fall with hunters, and in August with the Irish. Why they bought it God only knows," he shrugged. "He was in solid in Queens, so I suppose it was Natalie who wanted him out. Anyway, that's neither here nor there." He sat back. "This time of year they're slow, and I hear the food's not bad. It's only two weeks," he gestured. "You go—on me. It's the least I could do for Angelo's friends."

Margaret reddened. "We couldn't."

"Hey," he said with a smile. "I'm not offering you the Ritz. What's it gonna be, a coupla hundred dollars? I'll get one of the boys to drive you up—won't cost you a dime. What do you say? We old-timers got to stick together.''

Margaret hesitated.

"It's the only way to save your friend.''

"That's very kind of you,'' Margaret said finally. "Perhaps we should go.''

"Good.'' Donghia pushed his chair back from the table. "When can you be ready?''

Margaret thought for a moment. "This afternoon, I guess.''

"Five o'clock. Give me the address. And, if I were you, I wouldn't tell anyone where you're going.''

"Even my friends?''

"Nobody.''

"Okay.'' Margaret wrote out her address on a napkin and stood up. "Five o'clock.''

"Driver's name is Sol. You can trust him.''

Margaret smiled. "One of your bakers?''

"That's right,'' Donghia said with a grin. "He does the cookies.''

Thirty-eight

AT PRECISELY FIVE O'CLOCK THAT AFTER-noon a black stretch Fleetwood Cadillac pulled up to the curb in front of Margaret's building and left its motor idling. Behind the wheel, Sol DeFalco opened his new issue of *Guns and Ammo* and waited patiently for his pickup. He was absorbed in an article about the Walther PPK, a gun he was particularly fond of, when the rear door opened and an older woman stuck her head in.

"Sol?" she asked tentatively.

He nodded and put the magazine down. "Yeah."

"I wasn't expecting anything quite so grand," Margaret grinned. "Come on, Thelma, this is it." George, Margaret's doorman, brought the two large valises and put them in the trunk.

Twenty minutes later and a hundred yards before the turn-off to the George Washington Bridge, Sol pulled over to the side of the road and put on the parking brake. Cars whizzed by them and set the big Cadillac to rocking rhythmically. Sol was concentrating on the rearview mirror. Margaret leaned forward.

"Anything wrong?"

"Just checking. The boss said to make sure no one was following. If there is, they gotta pull over and I spot them or they miss the turn." After another two minutes, he took the brake off and eased out into traffic. He made the turn onto the bridge and increased his speed. "You can relax," he said. "We're clean."

They continued over the bridge, then headed north on the Palisades Parkway. The car, cruising at sixty-five miles an hour, felt like the Staten Island Ferry on a calm day.

"Be about two and a half hours," Sol said after a few minutes of silence. "There's a television set behind that center panel," he added, "but there's nothing much good on till the six o'clock news. I don't know what the reception's like up in the mountains."

"Thank you," Margaret said. After a few minutes, she leaned forward again. "Tell me, are you really a baker?"

Sol looked at her in the rearview mirror. "Twenty-two years next month. I started in a little place in Yorkville—lots of heavy dough. I didn't know about the featherlight touch until I came to Donghia's."

"You mind if I ask you something?" Margaret sat back into the soft upholstery. "How do you do a zeppole so it doesn't weigh a ton?"

"Ha!" Sol sank down into the seat more comfortably and smiled out at the road in front of him. "That's easy. You really want to know?"

"I've got two and a half hours," Margaret said, smiling. "Why waste it?"

Thirty-nine

NATALIE AND ANTHONY LANGRASCO were the least likely people Margaret could imagine running a small guest house in the mountains. Natalie reminded her of Alice Kramden in *The Honeymooners*, whereas her husband could have been one of Lee J. Cobb's flunkys in *On the Waterfront*. But they ran a lovely, clean inn and were friendly.

Margaret and Thelma approved of their room. A pair of white chintz covers lay over the twin beds and white ruffled curtains blew slightly in the breeze from the open window. A gaily colored hooked rug covered much of the space between the beds and matched the other two smaller rugs positioned in front of the pine chests. The old rose print wallpaper was only slightly faded.

"Lovely," Thelma said and looked around again. "I think I'm going to like it here." She went to the window and pulled a curtain to one side. Below her was the front lawn and then, across a little road, a large field with a border of pine trees. The light was fading, but she could still make out some lumbering shapes moving around in the gathering darkness.

"Cows," she said with a big grin. "Isn't that nice." She

turned back to her friend. "If the food is good, these two weeks will be wonderful."

"Well, let's go and see," Margaret said.

"Let me rest for just a minute. My arthritis seems to be acting up." She slowly opened and closed her hands a few times, wincing each time. She then sat down on the easy chair. Margaret began unpacking and in twenty minutes was finished. The two ladies then freshened up in the adjoining bath and went downstairs for dinner.

After the light supper of homemade minestrone soup and linguini, Thelma complained of a headache and went up to bed. Margaret insisted on helping Natalie and Anthony with the dishes.

"Mr. Donghia said to keep an eye on you," Anthony said casually as he was drying the large pot. "You in some kind of trouble?"

Natalie didn't look up, but Margaret could tell her attention was not solely on washing the forks.

"I don't think there'll be any problems," Margaret said slowly. "In two weeks we'll be back in the city and everything will be all right." She glanced over at Natalie who was now looking directly at her.

"Whatever it is, you just relax up here," the younger woman said. "The country is wonderful for making you see things more clearly." She took a quick look at her husband. "Stay as long as you need to. Anthony shouldn't have been so nosy." She took a step closer and took the drying rag from her husband's hand. "It's just that he used to be a young turk from Queens, and now he's drying dishes in Greene County. Sometimes he forgets that if he had stayed in Corona, old age would have been a luxury."

"Ha," Margaret smiled. "Old age is never a luxury. I like to think of it as a reward." She looked around. "I guess we're finished. The meal was delicious."

"Wait until tomorrow night," Anthony said. "Real country cooking."

Margaret raised an eyebrow. "Sugar glazed baked ham?"

"Lasagna." Natalie shrugged. "The Old Country."

Forty

AT TEN O'CLOCK THE NEXT MORNING, Schaeffer walked slowly down West Eighty-second Street until he was in front of Margaret's building. Morley had told him to check in—"make sure those two birds are all right." He turned into the small lobby and found himself facing an older man sitting leisurely in a faded armchair. If it hadn't been for the misshapen, visored cap, Schaeffer would have mistaken him for one of the tenants.

"You the doorman?"

The old man studied him with his rheumy eyes. "No, I like sitting in drafts."

Schaeffer grinned. "Margaret Binton in?"

The old man's eyes narrowed. The action forced moisture out onto the bridge of his nose. He took a second to wipe it away.

"Not here," he said. "Won't be back either. Not for a coupla weeks."

It was Schaeffer's turn to frown. "Where'd she go?"

"Dunno. Say," he leaned back, "why the interest all of a sudden? You're the second guy that's asked. I suppose you're her son, too?"

Schaeffer flashed his police identification. "Let's try it again. Now, what's this all about? Did the two ladies leave together?"

The doorman shrugged. "That's right—yesterday afternoon. Stepped into the biggest goddamn limo you ever saw."

"Limousine?"

"A regular battleship."

"And Mrs. Binton didn't say where she was going?"

"Nope. The two of 'em just waltzed out of here with grins on their faces and a suitcase each. I put the bags in the trunk. They waved goodbye and that was it."

"Did you get a license number?"

The man shook his head. "Sorry, the eyes ain't what they used to be."

"Grinning?" Schaeffer repeated.

"Like a pair of monkeys."

"What about the other guy, the one who said he was the son?"

"Came in yesterday afternoon. Except I'd bet a hundred they wasn't related."

"Why's that?"

"Puerto Rican," he said, "and Mrs. Binton's friend sounded like she was blue-blood Brooklyn."

"What'd he want?"

"Don't get me wrong. I got nothing against the Puerto Ricans—"

"What'd he want?" Schaeffer asked again with impatience.

When the doorman looked up again, his rheumy eyes seemed to have receded under new pools of liquid. "He said they didn't get along too well but that he was concerned about her health."

"Her health?"

"Yeah. He gave me a sawbuck. Told me he'd be by every day and if she needed help, I should tell him. You know—if she had to go to the hospital or something. I told him she seemed fine to me, but he sounded pretty sure she wasn't. The dough was as good in my pocket as it was in his, so I took it. He told me not to say a word to anyone, 'cept you're not anyone, you're a cop."

"Listen, when he comes around, you don't know anything—no limo, no trip, nothing. Got it? You play it that way and maybe Mrs. Binton and her friend will be all right. Now—'' Schaeffer pulled out a little pad—''what's this guy look like?''

The doorman gave him a warped smile. ''Like Carmen Miranda's son.''

Forty-one

''WHY THE HELL,'' MORLEY ASKED SCHAEFFER, ''does she have to pick on me? I rearrange my whole goddamn scheduling, and they take a powder on me. She couldn't phone me?''

Schaeffer tried to break in but Morley wasn't quite finished.

''The hell with it. If she wants to wind up a statistic, fine. I don't want to hear anymore about it. They're on their own now.'' He gulped his coffee and glared across the desk at Schaeffer.

''We can't just drop it, Sam. They're in a lot of trouble.''

''Yeah, well who told them to blow town like that?''

''Listen, you want to debate manners, okay. But it won't help them at all. Maybe she should'a called, but she didn't.'' Schaeffer took out a stick of gum and thrust it angrily in his mouth. He crumpled the wrapper and fired it overhand into the corner where it ricocheted off the two walls and landed in a wastebasket. ''Now I got a strong suspicion that someone's trying to kill Thelma Winters and you want to forget it? Sam, your brain is fried from overwork.''

Morley took another gulp of coffee. After some hesitation he nodded. "Okay, find her."

Forty-two

MARGARET AND THELMA HAD PLANNED A two-mile walk to the pond near Norton Hill but Thelma awoke in pain. The previous evening she'd had stomach cramps—trouble with the lasagna, she thought. But in the morning the pain was in her neck and joints, and she was so dizzy she could hardly stand. Margaret took her temperature and went downstairs to call a doctor. When she came back, Thelma's eyes were closed and she was holding her stomach and swallowing often. A tiny pleat of Thelma's red hair lay unattached as though it had been yanked from her head.

"My God!" Margaret said and saw Thelma open her eyes weakly.

"What is it?" she asked slowly.

"Nothing," Margaret stammered. "Go to sleep. I've asked the doctor to come and give you something for your arthritis."

Thelma studied her. "I think—" she began with great difficulty—"we shouldn't kid each other." Margaret covered her with another blanket, then went to the chair to wait.

An hour later, Margaret was still puzzling over how Thelma was being poisoned. The two friends had eaten the exact same foods for over a week, drunk the same beverages, and Margaret felt as healthy as ever. The sound of the arriving car intruded on her thoughts. "Thank goodness they still make house calls in Greene County,'' she said and hurried downstairs.

"You were right,'' Doctor Jamison said on the phone two hours later. "The blood tests were positive—it was poison. The hair loss was a giveaway. It's a rodenticide called thallium sulfite.''

Margaret clutched the phone tighter. "She'll be all right?''

"I think we've caught it in time. The activated charcoal I gave her will have absorbed any of the poison remaining in her stomach. The concentration in the blood is very high, but, at this moment, not fatal. It will take several days for her body to cleanse itself. There may be slight damage to the kidneys, but it's crucial that she not have another dosage. She's near the top as it is.''

"Is it possible,'' Margaret interrupted, "that she was poisoned several days ago and that it took that long for the symptoms to develop?''

There was silence on the other end of the phone for a few seconds.

"Possible,'' Doctor Jamison finally answered. "Yes, but the body reacts fairly quickly to thallium. From the levels in her body and from your description, I'd say she'd been ingesting it over the past few days also—slow buildup and chronic symptoms are different. We'll have to watch her diet closely. All it takes is one gram of absorbed thallium—''

"Watch her diet,'' Margaret said in exasperation. "It's the same as mine.''

Forty-three

WHEN KRAVITZ WAS SHOWN IN, FARRELL was seated behind the desk in his living room tapping the grip of a putter on the metallic edge in front of him. The other man walked nonchalantly to the couch, lit a cigar, and threw the extinguished match onto the table next to him. It landed nowhere near the large ashtray. Then he sat down and motioned with the burning cigar.

"Maybe I'm keeping you from something important?"

Farrell shook his head but said nothing. The other man eased himself back into the couch and stretched his legs in front of him. At six-foot-four inches, he looked like a ceiling timber fallen onto the couch. His expensively tailored blue sharkskin suit did not soften the image. His face was a map of past struggles, but his eyes were hooded and unrevealing. Only the fingers of his right hand drumming a stacatto beat on the leather of the cushion indicated his level of impatience. Or was it anger? Farrell waited.

"Nice place you got here."

"Yeah, I like it."

"You got some news for me?"

"News?"

"Quit cocking around. It's next week."

Farrell placed the putter against the wall slowly, then swiveled back. "That's right, September 21! Make sure you got the money ready. We'll need the million and a half to exercise the options on the adjoining property—they fall due the twenty-third.''

"Don't worry about *my* end," Kravitz said. "The money's been waiting for a long time." He pulled his leg in and flicked an ash off his knee. "Too long. The building empty yet?''

Farrell hesitated. "Yeah.''

"You don't sound very convincing. We gonna have a problem or what?''

"No one's living there. There's just one old lady that went to stay with a friend for a while. She's still paying rent—'' Farrell tried to smile but it came out as more of a leer. "But not for long.''

Kravitz held up a hand. "That's your business. All I need from you is an affidavit saying the building is empty and ready for conversion. I'll wire you the money the day I get it. But if I don't get the letter by Saturday, I'll be back for my original investment—with some friends," he added. "I sure hope you're liquid enough to come up with my five hundred grand. The last thing I want is to be the landlord of a slum tenement.''

"Look," Farrell said, leaning forward. "When we started three years ago we had nearly a full building—twenty apartments. Now we're down to one. You think that's bad? See if anybody else in this city could have done that. Now I got two parcels optioned, one on either side, and full plans for the entire complex. So stop pushing. It is a sure thing. If I tell you it's going to happen, it's going to happen—you'll get your affidavit.''

Kravitz eyed him carefully. "Everything else ready to go. Contractors, material?''

"Absolutely." Farrell reached out for the putter again. "Stop worrying. It's going to go as smooth as silk.''

Kravitz turned to go. "Remember, September 21.''

"Etched in cement," Farrell said.

"Yeah, let's hope not yours.''

Forty-four

TUESDAY WAS THE ONLY DAY THAT SID took a break from the horses. Grudgingly known as "dark day," it was the only time the New York tracks were closed. The OTB was handling out-of-town races, but Sid passed them up. Even God rested on the seventh day, he figured, but of course he'd done a perfect job of handicapping the other six. He bought himself coffee with a bagel for breakfast, greeted his friend at the newsstand, and then took his *Daily News* up to the Bliss Center. He spotted Schaeffer before he was two steps inside the large living room. The policeman was talking to Bertie, and both of them had anxious looks on their faces.

"What are you doing here?" Sid asked, sitting down next to them. "They're not supposed to let people under sixty in the door."

"Where's Margaret?" Schaeffer asked without smiling.

Sid was stung. "I dunno. I haven't seen her for days. Come to think of it, must be close to a week."

"Sergeant Schaeffer thinks she might be in trouble," Bertie said, leaning over. "She and Thelma went away together—in a limousine." She lingered over the last word.

"Sounds like the kind of trouble I'd like to be in. A limousine? Did she hit the lottery?"

"Who would they know with a car like that?" Schaeffer pressed.

"Rented?"

137

Schaeffer shook his head. "We checked. And it wasn't Farrell's either. He's got a Mercedes."

Sid rubbed his forehead. Schaeffer's anxiety was getting to him. "She's got no relatives around except a nephew in Jersey. But he lives in a tiny studio."

"So, who else could it be?" asked Bertie.

"Nobody. Far as I know, none of Margaret's friends got that kind of dough. Sorry." Sid leaned forward, frowning. "Unless it's that guy she went to see. The one that's connected with the mob." He turned to the officer next to him. "You know, the one Angelo got the gun from."

"Donghia?" Schaeffer said. "She went to see him?"

"Yeah, I'm sure. Maybe two weeks ago. The day after Angelo—"

"Thanks," Schaeffer said quickly and got up.

Bertie watched him go, then turned to Sid. "What's she doing going to the mob?"

"You think I know?" Sid said angrily. "She never tells me anything."

Forty-five

"IT'S VERY SERIOUS," DOCTOR JAMISON said looking down at Thelma. "She seems to have had a relapse. This morning her pulse is irregular and her motor reflexes are way off." He lifted Thelma's eyelid and looked into her eye. "Corneal reflex is slowing, too. We'll have to move her to the hospital."

Thelma groaned and a little shiver passed through her body. Margaret held her hand tighter.

"Can she hear us?" she asked.

"I don't think so. She's in a state of semiconsciousness."

"Buy why?" Margaret asked with a pained expression. "You said she was going to get better. That was two days ago."

"I know." Doctor Jamison put his instruments back in his case and quickly snapped it closed. "But she seems to have ingested more thallium. When I came last night she was almost normal."

"She was. She sat up and we watched television together."

The doctor reached for the phone. He dialed and asked for an ambulance. Then he turned back to Margaret. "Tell me what happened last night. Think carefully—did she eat anything, anything at all?"

"No, nothing but that soup you brought her." She pointed to the half-empty quart container on the bureau. "We each had a cup. She told me how much she liked split pea soup." Margaret held back a tear. "But that was all. I was watching very carefully. She had a glass of water before she went to bed, but it came from the tap. A few minutes later I had some, too—from the same tap. That's what's so strange, Doctor. I've never felt better in my life. How's she getting it?"

"Pills, medicines—?" queried Dr. Jamison.

"She doesn't use any! There are none around."

He shook his head. "Well, perhaps there was something you overlooked when she was in the bathroom alone."

"No!" Margaret said emphatically. "Nothing. The door was open, and I heard her wash her face and get the water. That was all." She squeezed Thelma's hand harder. "I feel so useless. She's dying in front of me, and there's nothing I can do. The window was locked from the inside and still is. I bolted the door." Margaret reached for a Kleenex as the tears finally came. After a minute she looked up again. "Doctor, you've got to save her. Coming here was my idea—none of this would have happened if I hadn't been so meddlesome. She'll be all right in the hospital, won't she?'' Margaret sounded unconvinced.

Doctor Jamison walked over to the container of soup and poured a little sample of it into a jar he found in his bag. "I'll have it analyzed," he said and slipped it into his pocket. Then he came over and sat down next to her. "I don't want to mislead you, Mrs. Binton. Mrs. Winters is in a grave condition. She's an old woman and her body can put up with just so many continued assaults of this poison. There were residual levels of thallium in her blood even when she seemed better. Her chances, I would say, are modest at best. The poison has to be gotten out of her body within three or four hours, before too much more is absorbed. I'm sorry.''

There were footsteps in the hall followed by a knock on the door. Two paramedics came in, strapped Thelma in place, and in four minutes they were all gone. The only noise in the room was the steady hum that came from the electric clock on the night table. The dial said 11:30 A.M. Trying hard to concentrate, Margaret went over and sat on her unmade bed.

Let's take it from the beginning, she thought. Jamison's last visit was at 5:00 P.M. What did we do from then on—minute by minute. There was something, some wispy shred of fact nagging at her. For almost two hours she tried to pinpoint it. At the end of that time she was startled by a familiar voice.

"Open up Margaret. Are you there?''

She got up quickly and opened the door. "David, what are you doing here?''

Sergeant Schaeffer took a step into the room and held her by the shoulders. He looked inquisitively at her face.

"You all right?''

"It's not me, it's Thelma," Margaret said. "They took her to the hospital a little while ago—poison. Now do me a favor and sit down over there.'' She pointed to the easy chair. "I just had something—''

"Wait a minute," Schaeffer interrupted.

"Shhh,'' Margaret said. "It's something about the bathroom.'' She walked over and stood at the door frame, looking inside. Schaeffer walked up behind her.

''Errors of commission and errors of omission,'' she said softly. ''Yes, that's what it was!'' She twirled around. ''I knew there was something funny—it's not what she did, it's what she *didn't* do.''

''What the hell are you talking about?'' Schaeffer said.

''I reviewed in my mind very carefully what Thelma did last night, and I paid special attention to what she did in the bathroom. That was the only time she was out of my sight— but I heard. I told Doctor Jamison I heard her wash her face and drink a glass of water.''

''So?''

''So, I didn't hear her brush her teeth. In fact, I've never heard her brush her teeth, even in New York when she was living with me. Now don't you think that's peculiar?''

Schaeffer shrugged. ''There have been times when I've forgotten.''

''Not for two whole weeks. And there was something else. Thelma was always going to bed after me. It's something you don't notice unless you think about it and see a pattern. She would always read until I was dozing, and then she would go into the bathroom. By the time she came out, I was usually asleep, or, at the very least, had my eyes closed. Now,'' Margaret took a step into the bathroom, ''why was that?''

Schaeffer frowned. ''She wore a wig and didn't want you to see her without it.''

''No, but that's close. I think she was embarrassed, but not about her hair. That was real enough.'' She bent down and removed a tiny little smear of red paste from the sink near the stopper. She looked at it closely, then rubbed it between her fingers. ''No, not her hair, her teeth—as false as Scarlett O'Hara's waistline. I use Colgate. This''— she held out her fingers—''is something else, and I think I know what. Come on.'' She turned back quickly into the room. ''Help me with this suitcase. Thelma kept a few things inside, and maybe it's there.''

Sergeant Schaeffer pulled the suitcase from the closet floor

and laid it on the bed. Margaret grabbed the zipper and
yanked, the two halves opening like a split apple, disclosing
some dirty clothes and unread books on both sides. Plunging
her hand underneath, Margaret searched through them. After
a few seconds, she stopped and withdrew her right hand. In
it was a peculiarly shaped plastic cup, and this she tossed on
the bed. After another half-minute of rummaging, she gave
up.

"Well, that's half of it," she said. "But the paste—" She
began opening drawers in the bureau and looking in the
pockets of Thelma's clothes. She was about to start over
again on the suitcase when she moved the Bible in Thelma's
nightstand drawer. Underneath it, was the half-used tube of
paste.

"Here it is," she cried and placed it next to the cup. "Poor
Thelma," she sighed. "Hiding it like that—as if I cared."

"Denture adhesive," Schaeffer said slowly, picking up the
red-and-white tube.

"And a soaking cup," Margaret added. "For cleaning her
false teeth at night. Now I understand why she always went
to bed after me—she had her teeth out and in her cup. She
probably put them on the floor by her bed at night. In the
morning, she would quickly put on a strip of paste and insert
them. She did it so well that she fooled me all this time."
Margaret reached for the tube and opened it. A minty odor
reached her nose, an odor strong enough to mask another,
more foreign substance. "I'll bet the thallium is in here,"
Margaret said and closed the tube. "We've got to hurry.
What time is it?"

"Almost 2:00 P.M."

"I'll call first, but then I've got to bring this to Doctor
Jamison. I hope it's not too late. How'd you get here?"

"By car."

"Good. I just hope the town of Leeds knows about
sirens."

The hospital in Catskill, New York, was a modern,
multistoried building set pleasantly in a residential neighborhood. Margaret and Schaeffer quickly found the intensive

care unit and managed to get one of the nurses to page Doctor Jamison. In two minutes he came through the glass doors that led from the unit.

"I took the plate out," he said quickly to Margaret. "The test showed a concentration of almost a quarter of a gram of thallium. She must have just put in the plate with fresh adhesive this morning. You have the tube it came from?"

Margaret fished in her purse and gave it to him. As she did she held onto his hand.

"How is she?"

"We're holding her. Another couple of hours with that plate in her mouth and she'd be dead for sure. Absorption through the mucous membranes of the mouth is very fast, and I'm not even considering what leaked into her stomach. If she pulls through, she'll be a lucky woman. We would have found it sooner or later, but most likely during the autopsy." He hesitated for a moment. "Why didn't she say anything about it when she was getting sicker?"

"I don't think she wanted anybody to know. She put a lot of effort into concealing it. Also, at first she must have thought the pain was only her arthritis acting up. May I go in and see her?"

"I'm afraid not. Come back this evening. The next few hours will be critical."

"Doctor Jamison," Margaret said slowly. "If she does recover, will there be any permanent damage?"

The doctor didn't answer at first. "I don't know," he said finally. "We'll have to see."

Forty-six

FIVE DAYS LATER, SEPTEMBER 19, SCHAEFFER opened the front door of Margaret's apartment building and walked straight for the doorman. The old man was sitting at the little desk studying an old issue of *Cosmopolitan* and didn't trouble to look up. Schaeffer tossed his badge onto the lingerie ad the old man was reading so carefully.

"Remember me?" Schaeffer waited. "It was only a week ago."

The doorman looked up and wiped his eyes with a disheveled handkerchief. Then he shot a look down at the badge.

"Yeah, how could I forget? You find Mrs. Binton and her friend?"

Schaeffer nodded. "They're outside," he said slowly. "We need you for the door."

The old man lifted himself heavily off his seat. He was about to pass Schaeffer when Schaeffer put a hand out.

"Your friend been back?"

"Who's that?"

"The guy who was asking about Mrs. Winters's health— the one who gave you the ten dollars."

The doorman snorted. "Every day. Some days I tell him I ain't seen her. Other days I tell him she's looking okay. Threw me a couple more bills, but I didn't let on they wasn't in."

They walked to the front door, and the older man held it open. Schaeffer motioned outside. "When he comes back again, you can tell him he was right. Mrs. Winters is—" he hesitated—"very sick." Schaeffer nodded at the checker taxi cab with the wheelchair being lifted out of the side door. "Very sick," he repeated. In a minute the taxi driver pushing the wheelchair passed by, and Schaeffer glanced down at a groaning Thelma, her complexion the color of oatmeal and her eyes rimmed with gray. The doorman looked down and shook his head.

"Jesus! What happened?"

Margaret followed her friend into the lobby. "We don't know," Margaret said carefully. "She just started getting worse and worse."

"Just like that?" The older man looked skeptical.

Schaeffer tapped his shoulder as Margaret followed the driver to the elevators. "If that guy comes back, you just tell him she's very sick and may not make it. Forget about everything else." Schaeffer took a quick glance at the street outside just in case Geraldo was there watching. "And don't get too elaborate or you might make a mistake."

"Sure." The doorman smiled and let go of the door. It closed with the metallic sound of a jail cell. "I'll tell him anything you say." He walked back to his seat and looked down at the magazine. "I seen a lot of strange things in my forty years," he mumbled.

Schaeffer passed the taxi driver coming back from the elevators and gave him the fare plus a big tip. After some jockeying around, Margaret, Schaeffer, and Thelma squeezed into the elevator. The old doorman watched the doors close, then adjusted his visored cap and looked back down at the glossy pages.

Schaeffer left an hour later, nodding curtly to the doorman as he passed by.

"How's she doing?" the old man asked matter of factly.

"Not good," Schaeffer said. "Don't forget the message."

"I didn't." He leaned back. "Fella came by fifteen minutes ago." Schaeffer stopped. "Didn't I tell you I knew he ain't her son?"

"Why's that?" Schaeffer asked.

"He didn't even ask about her. Gave me the saddest look I ever seen manufactured and almost tripped on the door sill in his hurry to get out. Now, does that sound right to you?"

Schaeffer reached for the door. "Maybe he couldn't stand the responsibility. What time you go off?"

"In a coupla hours—at 4:00 PM."

Schaeffer came back into the lobby and handed the old man a crumpled bill. "Here, buy yourself a beer on your way home. You deserve it." He turned to go.

"Hey, tell me something. How come the cops are involved? It's only an old lady."

"Maybe one day it'll be an old man." Schaeffer walked away, leaving the doorman staring at the piece of paper in his hand.

"Whaddya know," the man murmured. "Mr. Hamilton himself!"

Forty-seven

WHEN THE DOORMAN CAME IN ONE HOUR late the next morning with his head as heavy as a waterlogged stump and his memory as wispy as a Jersey fog, a city Health Department ambulance was already double-parked in front of the door. Shortly thereafter, a middle-aged man with a medic's valise emerged from the elevator followed by Margaret Binton. Her eyes were red and she looked as if she hadn't slept all night.

"I'm sorry, Mrs. Binton," the man said with a note of

impatience. "There's not a thing anyone can do except call a funeral parlor. If there's not enough money I'll arrange for a morgue pickup."

"No," Margaret cried. "Not that. Oh God, not the morgue." She turned and saw the doorman. "Oh, George—" She put a hand out and burst into tears again.

"Take care of her," the man with the valise said. "I've given her a mild sedative. It should calm her down. Get her upstairs."

The doorman nodded and held onto her hand. At his touch, Margaret seemed to collect herself and wiped her eyes.

"It was so awful," she said. "She started gasping then all of a sudden she just stopped breathing—nothing I could do."

The older man led her back to the elevator. "Want me to bring you upstairs?"

"Thank you."

Guiding her inside he held onto her until they reached the front door of her apartment.

"Could you close the door to the bedroom?" she asked and went to sit on her couch. George took the few steps over and grabbed the knob. He looked inside, shuddering at what he saw. There, on one of the beds, was a shapeless form with a sheet pulled over its head. One inert arm hung limply to the side. The only movement in the room came from a dimity curtain that floated on the light gusts of air from the window. George pulled the door tight and wiped his mouth.

"Terrible," he said and turned back to Margaret. He steadied himself on the door frame.

Margaret sniffed. "I should call someone about the funeral—thank you, George. So many of my friends have died that I should be used to this by now." She got up and walked to the phone. "Except that each time is like the first time."

The doorman left quickly, closing the door behind him. The last thing he saw was Margaret talking to someone softly on the phone.

Meanwhile, Geraldo watched closely as the man with the valise crossed the street. He had been waiting since 8:00 that morning for something to happen, so he'd seen the ambu-

lance pull up forty-five minutes earlier. He left his spot in a
doorway a dozen yards away and sauntered up near the ambulance. Just then, the man carrying the valise opened the
door next to the driver and flung himself in. Shaking his
head, he picked up the microphone on the dashboard radio.

"This is Jacobson," he said in a voice loud enough to
reach Geraldo. "Call 4538—Caucasian female, early seventies, name, Thelma Winters. Dead on arrival. Death oc-
curred at 7:00 A.M. from pulmonary edema. No assistance
possible or medication given. We're on to the next one,
4539." He hung the microphone up and motioned to the
driver. "Let's go."

Geraldo headed for Margaret's building, a look of anticipation in his eyes. He walked inside and cornered the doorman.

"I saw the ambulance," he said quickly. "She's dead?"

The old man's head was throbbing. Slumping in his chair,
he said simply, "Yeah, she's dead." He made a gesture with
his hand. "I saw the body myself. Had a sheet over her head."

"No mistake?" Geraldo asked.

"Get the hell out of here," George said angrily. "Son-of-
a-bitch. Got no respect for the dead."

Geraldo ran into the street and to the first telephone booth
he saw.

Farrell put the phone down lightly and leaned back. Looking
out the window at the green vista of Central Park, broken at
intervals by the sheen of water, he permitted a smile to cross
his face. He'd done it—an empty building. And no way to
prove he had anything to do with the old lady's death. Luther
was dead. Geraldo had never see him. They could threaten
him all they wanted, but they had no case. He reached forward and pushed a button on his intercom. When the young
secretary entered the room, Farrell motioned to the seat.

"Come in, Gloria—this telex is to Mr. Kravitz. 'Re mortgage agreement between Mayberry Mews and Financial Diversified Industries Corporation, I herewith notify you that the
property at 621 West Ninety-first Street is, as of today, Sep-

tember 20, empty of all tenants and is available for demolition. Under the terms of the agreement, I request that your existing mortgage be increased by $1,500,000 and that the funds be sent to me promptly.' '' He stopped and thought for a moment. "Gloria, change that to 'immediately.' '' He smiled.

Forty-eight

"YOU WHAT?" MORLEY LOOKED UNBElievingly at Schaeffer who was sitting stiffly in front of him. "Tell me again. I don't believe this."

Schaeffer cautiously rubbed a finger behind his ear and waited a moment.

"I—um—borrowed Jacobson and Staunton this morning." He held the same hand up to ward off a further comment from Morley. "Now wait. I know what you're going to say. They were supposed to be on the arson case, but this was more important. Geraldo would have spotted me in a minute. Besides, it was only for an hour."

"Only for an hour! Even if it was for one goddamn minute. I'm supposed to be in charge here."

"I understand that," Schaeffer said calmly. "But it just had to be done. Someone had to be the medic, and someone had to be the driver of the ambulance."

"Wait a minute," Morley motioned with his hand. "Back up a bit. Who the hell is Geraldo and *what* ambulance?"

"You remember—" Schaeffer looked surprised—"the super in Mrs. Winters's building."

"Winters, Winters?" Morley frowned trying to place the name.

"Margaret's friend."

"Jesus Christ!" Morley exploded. "What the hell do you think you're doing?" His face was red. "Since when are you making the assignments around here?"

Schaeffer shook his head. "If you want to calm down and listen, that's one thing. If you want to bust me," he raised his shoulders, "that's your privilege."

Morley took a breath. "This better be good."

"Actually, it was Margaret's idea, but she needed me for the men and the ambulance." He grinned. "The wheels took a little doing, and then I had to promise the guys down at Murphey's office a pair of tickets to the first Jets game. Besides that, it won't cost the taxpayers a thing."

Morley sat down slowly. "From the top," he said. "And if I don't like it," he added, "start packing."

Forty-nine

ONE WEEK LATER, A NEW YORK CITY PO-
lice patrol car pulled up in front of Farrell's Central Park West apartment building with its lights flashing. Schaeffer was driving and on his right was Lieutenant Morley. When the car stopped moving Morley turned to look at their passengers in the rear seat. Margaret Binton returned his attention with a friendly smile.

"Don't worry," she said. "We'll be perfectly all right." She turned to the woman next to her. "Won't we, dear?"

Thelma was dressed in a tight-fitting tweed suit and a beige blouse that contrasted favorably with her ruddy cheeks. Her prized red hair was much thinner from the thallium and had been combed out into a loose pageboy. A sweet little pin in the shape of a parrot sat on her collar.

"Oh, my, yes. I'm sure Mr. Farrell will understand. I don't think he'll do anything rash with David there." She felt in her handbag until her fingers grasped the piece of paper. "I have the check, I guess we can go."

Sergeant Schaeffer stepped out of the car and walked around to the curbside door. "Did you tell him you were coming?" Schaeffer asked Margaret as she emerged from the car.

She shook her head. "Best to surprise him—much more effective."

The three of them walked into the building and stopped by the chrome switchboard.

"Jason Farrell, please," Thelma said cautiously to the doorman.

"Who should I say is calling?" he intoned.

"Just say," Margaret interrupted, "a business associate of Mr. Kravitz." She held Thelma's hand.

In a minute the doorman turned back to them. "You may go up." He motioned in the direction of the elevators.

As they entered, Margaret turned toward Schaeffer.

"Let me do all the talking."

Schaeffer grinned. "It's your show, yours and Thelma's."

The elevator opened, and the little group faced Farrell's entry door. Without hesitation, Margaret rang the bell. The door was opened by an attractive woman who ushered them inside. Margaret remembered the apartment-office from her last visit. This time, however, there was no manicurist—and no Luther. Farrell was sitting all alone at his desk. When he looked up his features hardened and he glanced questioningly at his secretary, then back to Margaret.

"You! What do you want?" He allowed himself a second to study her two friends.

Margaret sat down, and directed Thelma and Schaeffer to two of the other chairs.

"First, let me introduce my friend Sergeant Schaeffer to you—Eighty-first Precinct. I'm sure you appreciate the fine work they do. His boss, Lieutenant Morley is downstairs in their squad car. If you care to look out of your window, it's the one with the little red flashing light."

Schaeffer flashed his shield in case Farrell had any doubts.

"I only mention that in case you harbor any doubts about how serious we are, or, what is more to the point, how seriously you should take us. Now then," she turned to Thelma, "I suppose you two have never met. Imagine that."

Farrell regarded Thelma but his expression held steady. There was not even the slightest glint of suspicion in his face. Just another old lady, he thought.

"This is the woman you tried to kill," Margaret said. "As you can see, Mrs. Winters is quite alive and healthy. She's come, upon my suggestion, to pay her next month's rent in person." Margaret nodded to her friend. "Thelma, put the check on Mr. Farrell's desk. It's made out to Mantex but we thought it might as well go directly to its destination." She sat back and smiled politely.

Farrell stared at Thelma. "What is this, some joke? Thelma Winters is dead." He looked at Margaret. "Did you bring in some ringer or what?"

"You shouldn't believe everything you hear," Thelma said in a quiet voice. "There are at least a dozen ways I can prove who I am. As far as my 'death' is concerned, it's quite amazing what a little makeup can do. That and some first-class acting." She turned to Margaret and patted her hand.

"Which brings us to Mr. Kravitz," Margaret added.

"What the hell do you have to do with Kravitz?" Farrell asked softly. He was doing his best to stay in control.

"Well, by now I suspect you have used his additional million and a half dollars and exercised the options on the adjacent properties." Margaret smiled. "If I'm not mistaken, the expiration date was three days ago. In that case, Mr. Farrell, I'd say you were in a rather awkward position—given Mrs. Winters's healthy condition, that is. Parking lots at $2 million are somewhat overpriced, even for this city. And I can only guess how your partner, Mr. Kravitz, would feel about such an inefficient use of his money. Oh, don't worry," she added, "I'll make sure he finds out."

Farrell slammed the table with his fist. The sudden action brought Schaeffer to his feet with his hand inside his coat pocket. The two men glowered at each other.

"Let's have no more outbursts," Schaeffer said. "Makes me nervous. Besides," he said slowly, "it's impolite."

"Son-of-a-bitch, Kravitz will kill me."

"Perhaps a little melodramatic," Margaret said. "My guess is he'll make it very difficult for you to continue your business." She looked around. "You might even have to give up all this."

"Listen to me," Farrell said in an almost pleading way, "I'll be a sitting duck." He turned to Schaeffer. "You tell them. You know what they're like."

Schaeffer just shrugged and stretched his legs.

"You can't do this." Farrell clenched the back of the chair.

"You should have thought of that beforehand," Thelma said in such a cold, cutting voice that Margaret looked at her for a moment. "Before the others, and especially before Angelo."

Margaret interrupted. "However, there is a way we might be able to help. We've talked about it, and Mrs. Winters has indicated she might be persuaded to move. That would accomplish what you want and, if the location were the right one, it would suit Mrs. Winters, also."

Farrell took a deep breath and nodded slowly.

"I should have figured. There's always some goddamn angle."

"No," Margaret said. "Urban relocation. The city's doing it all the time."

Silence filled the room. "Okay, let's hear it," Farrell finally said. "Where?"

"Sixteen A, Westhaven Tower."

"What!" Farrell rose out of his chair. "The three-bedroom penthouse duplex with the wrap terrace and Jacuzzi. You're crazy."

"Mrs. Winters," Margaret said simply, "likes space, trees,

light, and warm baths. It's perfect for her. And I happen to know it's still empty. Mrs. Winters would be happy to reclaim the rent check she just handed you if you make out a signed contract on 16 A for the sum of one dollar." Margaret rummaged through her large handbag. "Yes, here it is. I took the liberty of taking a blank contract the first day I visited your sales office. It's all made out." She tossed it on the desk next to Thelma's check. "It's your move, Mr. Farrell."

Farrell closed his eyes, remaining that way for some time.

"Three G," he said. "Very nice layout—one bedroom, efficiency kitchen. It's listed at one hundred ninety thousand dollars. I could sell it tomorrow for one and a half. Take it, it's yours for a buck. Just get out of 621 West Ninety-first."

Margaret shook her head and rose from her chair. "Sixteen A, Mr. Farrell, nothing else. We can go floor by floor if you want, apartment by apartment, but the answer will still be the same—16 A or Thelma goes back home."

Farrell's face turned an angry red. He pointed a finger at Thelma. "You're turning down one hundred and fifty thousand dollars to go back to a rat-infested, crumbling, paint-chipped apartment. Who are you trying to kid?"

"Let's go, Thelma," Margaret said and stood up. Thelma followed.

"Hold it," he said. "I'll make it the A apartment. But the eighth floor, not the penthouse."

Margaret turned the handle on the door. "You know our offer. It's a shame you're not taking us seriously." She pulled it open.

"Okay," he said. "Okay, you got it. Sixteen A—the penthouse."

Margaret released the knob. "That's better," she said taking a step back into the room. "Now, if you'd sign your contract, I'm sure you'd like to see Mrs. Winters rip up her check. Yes, that's right, sign right underneath where it says, 'one dollar.' And you will see I've added a clause saying you will be responsible for common charge and property taxes."

Reluctantly, Farrell leaned forward, picked up his gold ballpoint pen, and brought it over to the contract. He shook his head, took a final look at Thelma, and signed. "So much for New York City's finest—a cop sitting in the room and party to an outright swindle—witnessing it no less."

"What swindle?" Schaeffer asked innocently. "All I heard was Mrs. Winters offering to pay her October rent on a place she's lived in for forty-two years. You're the one offering to move her."

"Bah!" Farrell stood up and grabbed the two pieces of paper. "Here, take them."

Walking over to the desk, Thelma reached out and took the check and the contract. Her hand shook as she brought them up to eye level. After a minute of studying the contract, she faced him.

"What you did to our building, Mr. Farrell, was a crime. Before you came, twenty families lived together, and we had our own little neighborhood inside our building. Like a small village somewhere, we all shared. But you destroyed that little community and you committed murder. Angelo was my close friend, and you had him killed with less emotion than you'd show for a sick dog." She started to cry but continued. "Then you tried to kill me. And now you're buying your way out. I thought I could take your offer, but it won't work. I can't," she said, raising her chin, "let you get away with it." She tore the contract in half and continued ripping the paper until it was in little pieces on the carpet. "I won't be bought out. Here, Mr. Farrell, is my rent check." She placed it back down on his desk and turned to Margaret. "Let's go. It's about time I went home." Without looking back, she walked to the door and passed through.

"No," Farrell shouted after her. "He'll kill me!"

Margaret got up, took Schaeffer's arm, and trailed after her friend.

Farrell's shouts followed them into the elevator.

About the Author

Richard Barth is a goldsmith and an assistant professor at the Fashion Institute of Technology. He lives in Manhattan with his wife and two children. THE CONDO KILL is the first book in the Margaret Binton mystery series.